Painting Gluttony

Erin Coal

Erin Coal

Painting Gluttony

ISBN: 9798375495996

Erin Coal

Also by Erin Coal:

Seven Deadly Sins Series

Writing Wrath

Painting Gluttony

Solving Greed

Night Coven Duology

Sacrifice

Vengeance

Erin Coal

Playlist

1. Jennifer Lopez- After Love

2. Labrinth- Beneath Your Beautiful

3. Violent Femmes- Good Feeling

4. Red Hot Chili Peppers- Under the Bridge

5. The Weekend- Blinding Lights

6. Green Day- Time of Your Life

7. Muse- Feeling Good

8. Florence + the Machine- Never Let Me Go

9. Incubus- Wish You Were Here

10. Kanye West- Stronger

Erin Coal

Painting Gluttony

CHAPTER ONE
Laurel

"If I make this shot, I get to decide where we go tonight," Bella suggests as she swings her legs from my desk, holding one of my discarded and screwed-up pieces of notepaper in her hand. She motions to a tiny bin at the opposite end of the room, a literal long shot.

"You normally decide that anyway," I snort, trying to focus on the notepad in front of me.

"But this time, I can take you anywhere I want," she waggles her eyebrows at me, and I can't help but laugh. Bella had long, glossy blonde hair, and blue eyes and was so petite she was often described as fairy-like. She was also completely secure with her sexuality and was an open dominatrix at a local BDSM club, Seven Deadly Sins. She had asked me several times to go, but I nervously declined.

"That sounds like I'm going to wake up in a bathtub missing a kidney," I laugh, re-reading the same line of the case file for the third time before giving up—my concentration has officially gone. "Fine, I'm in," I conceded. I watched as the white ball of paper sailed through the air and landed smoothly inside its target.

"Yes!" Bella cried, I rolled my eyes at her. "Wear something sexy!" She told me, throwing herself off my desk and flouncing towards the door.

"I'm still not sure about this," I call after her, nerves and excitement warring inside me.

"Come to my place first then I'll teach you everything you need to know," she hollers as my doorbell tinkles behind her like it's laughing at me. The thought of going to some kind of BDSM club always unsettled me a little, unsure why people wouldn't keep any dark desires between themselves and their partner. I wasn't a prude, I just believed that some parts of a relationship should be private, but my track record told me I obviously wasn't taking the right approach in the past. My landline ringing broke me out of my thoughts.

"Slater's Solicitors," I say as formally as I can, feeling really out of practice at this stuff as I got way too used to having someone to do this for me in my old life, and it feels like I'm taking a crash course in relearning this stuff.

"Um, hi," comes a timid-sounding female voice. "I need some help with my divorce." The poor woman sounds terrified.

"I can help you with that," I reassure her.

"But I don't want my husband to know I'm filing for divorce until I have the rest sorted."

"The rest?" Silence greets my question, and I feel an anxious squeeze in my throat. "Tell me everything, and I'll do whatever I can to help," I tell her earnestly. I have an uncontrollable urge to help people even when it goes way beyond what I should do to help them, and this woman instantly had me wanting to do anything to help her.

"My name is Stephanie, and I'm in a really bad situation," she tells me with a resigned sigh. I pull my notepad and pen towards

me again, and I start furiously scribbling notes as she tells me
her tragic tale.

Two hours later, I'm dressed and ready to go, my mind still
whirling over what Stephanie had told me and how I was going
to help her escape her awful husband. No one should put up
with a living situation like that. No one. I was supposed to be
back in Rhyl to avoid trouble, and here I was, running into it
head-first again. I shook my head, making my carefully styled
brunette curls rustle against the fabric of my tiny black dress. I
tugged my dress down at the back again, which I would probably
end up doing most of the night with my huge arse that never
seemed to fit into anything properly, and threw on a parka over
the top to keep the February chill off my skin. I grabbed my car
keys and a container with the extra chilli and rice I had for
dinner and headed down the stairs and out the door of my flat,
handily situated above my shop.

The door to my flat spilt out onto a tiny parking lot, just enough
for myself and my neighbours to park a single car each and
squeeze in and out of the spaces before joining a side street to
circle back to the main road. I eyed my tiny Ford KA with a sigh,

the dull silver paint mocking me as I strode towards it. I had loved the huge Range Rover I'd had before I moved back here— the seats had been made of buttery leather and heated. Selling it to use the cash to start my practice here had felt like a physical wound, the tiny and ancient car that had been all I could afford had been like rubbing salt into the wound.

"Hey Melvin," I called, finally spotting him sheltering between the two huge recycling bins that served all the flats.

"Hey!" He called, standing up from his sleeping bag on the ground to greet me. The sight of his sleeping arrangement made my heart pang with guilt about how much I still had in my life and how ungrateful I was being. I had met Melvin a couple of days after moving in, quickly finding out he had been over in Afghanistan when he had been shot in the leg, and just couldn't acclimatise to being back home again after everything he had seen and done. He refused to take any kind of charity or help, but I had convinced him to let me bring him a hot meal when I had extra.

"Got you some chilli and rice tonight," I smiled, handing the container over. He opened the container and sniffed it, letting out a hum of pleasure.

"Smells delicious. Thank you so much!" He exclaimed, and I couldn't help but smile that I had been able to help someone today. "You look pretty, going out?"

"Yeah, just out with Bella again, be safe tonight, Melvin," I told him, heading towards my car.

"You too, Laurel!" He called as I dropped into the drivers seat. I drew in a steadying breath as I started the engine, trying to brace myself for whatever tonight was going to bring.

CHAPTER TWO

Laurel

"You need to loosen up," Bella's voice carried over the top of my car as we both stepped out of it, "really lose yourself in orgasmic pleasure and let yourself go." I frantically looked around for anyone who might overhear our conversation, this was a new world for me, and I was both exhilarated and embarrassed.

"I can't believe I let you talk me into this," I glared at my friend for what felt like the thousandth time tonight as she began leading me across the creepy and silent car park that stretched out around us, only faintly lit by a few dim street lights dotted around. I spotted where she was leading me; towards a warehouse that looked slightly terrifying in the darkness. If I hadn't known her better, I would think she brought me here to murder me.

"Laurel, you're wound so tight I'm worried one orgasm might make you pass out," she snorted. "I won our little bet today, so I get the honour of trying to get your workaholic arse to have some fun!" Bella's voice still felt way too loud and carried across the empty car park, but she had always been way more confident than me. The warehouse we were walking towards glared back at me whilst I tried to reign in my nervous trembles and stay upright in my heels on the gravel car park.

The whole BDSM thing hadn't even been on my radar until I moved back to Rhyl two months ago and reconnected with Bella. After what she perceived as a bland life in Manchester, my high school best friend had been a well-needed, colourful dose of medicine. I tried to put my trust in her about this club too. Bella strutted into the warehouse and through the reception area. It looked like we were in a normal office building, which sent a small tremor of panic through me until Bella swiped her card and received a green light of approval from the reader. This was definitely the right place. Two beefy men sat behind the reception desk and nodded in greeting to us as we walked past, Bella's wheely case squeaking slightly on the wooden floor. I followed her down a long corridor painted jet black, but she yanked me into a hidden side room just before two large double doors. Lockers lined the walls, and there was a bench with coat hooks down the middle, which reminded me of a gym changing room.

"So, if someone asks if you are a sub or a Domme, what do you say?" Bella quizzes me as she unzips her wheelie case and begins to change into what looks like a large pile of belts.

"I say it's my first time here, and I don't know what I enjoy," I recite back to her for the fifth time. When she suggested we come here, she made it sound light-hearted and fun before lecturing me for the last hour on rules and protocols.

"And if someone asks you to play, what are the check-in words?" she had stripped naked while we were talking, not feeling any need to be modest. I focused on an interesting spot on the ceiling, feeling way out of my depth now, my comfort zone somewhere outside in the car park.

"Green means happy to carry on, amber means things are a bit too intense, so slow down or ease up, and red means stop right that second," I repeated the words she had made me memorise. "Good, you are officially ready!" Bella exclaimed, pulling out a riding crop from the case that made me nervous. I warily lowered my eyes to see the pile of belts had become a very revealing dress that left lots of skin on show but had buckles over the right places, showing off her mesmerising curves whilst retaining some modesty. Stowing the case and my coat in one of the changing room lockers, Bella took my hand and tugged me towards the double doors. I drew in a steadying breath, unsure what would await me on the other side of the double doors, but hell, I was here—I may as well give it a try. Who knows, I might even like it.

The first thing that strikes me as we enter is how nice the room is. I had expected dingy and tacky but not the ornate white and gold that surrounded us. There were several small groups of people clustered on sofas and chairs scattered through the large room, happily chatting away like this was a normal social event. Which it could have been if everyone weren't wearing underwear, PVC or leather, accessorised with whips, ball gags and collars around their necks. A loud crack followed by a yelp drew my attention across the room. A huge, muscled, red haired man had a small, naked, blonde woman upside down and over his knee as he continued mercilessly spanking her upturned arse cheeks, the simultaneous cracks echoing across the room. Her thighs were trapped under one of his legs, the rest of her held upside down by one of his strong arms. I couldn't help but stare at the jiggling red cheeks as they took blow after blow. I was mesmerised by her glistening arousal that was glaringly obvious, as I began to get turned on too.

"Do you want to be the man or the woman?" Bella asked from beside me. I must have given her a confused look as she explained: "do you picture yourself as the one giving the spanking or the one being spanked?"

"I wish I was the woman," I answered softly, confirming what she had already suspected, that I would prefer to be submissive than to be the Dominant one. My day job meant I was bossy and domineering, so it made sense I suppose, that I craved a rest from that and a change of pace in my sex life.

"Cool, so we are looking for a Dom for you then," Bella shrugged, leading me towards one of the empty sofas. "Would you prefer a male or female Dom/Domme, or are you open?" The blonde woman was still receiving more harsh spanks to her behind, and I noticed another female sub across from them who was furiously licking between her mistresses spread legs, receiving words of encouragement.

"I'm open," I tell her, barely above a whisper. Everyone just carried on like this was perfectly normal to be going on around them, whereas I had no idea what to do with myself and where to look; my body flushed with heat, arousal and embarrassment. Bella, on the other hand, was smiling calmly as she watched me take all this in. While I was tugging my short black dress down to cover my huge arse that was spilling out again, now I was sat down.

"Calm down—you're going to hyperventilate," she laughed. "Most people in a scene out here wouldn't mind if you joined in, just don't forget to ask for permission first." Her words brought a furiously embarrassed flush to my cheeks. "Just don't go in any of the sin rooms or private rooms if the doors are closed. That means people really don't want anyone watching their scene or making it into an orgy."

"Bella!" I gasped, unable to contain my embarrassment. A man's shaved head appeared on her lap before she could reply and began rubbing his cheek against her thigh in a cat-like gesture. "Good evening, Mistress," he purred as Bella began stroking his head affectionately. My eyes roved over his handsome form. He was almost naked, apart from a pair of tight PVC shorts and a slim leather collar around his neck. From where I was sitting, I could tell how aroused he was already—he looked like he had a tin can down his pants, held prominently in place by the unyielding material.

"Hello, little one," Bella affectionately cooed while I watched the exchange, fascinated. She had already explained to me that she and this man were exclusive play partners, but they didn't have a clue what each other's surnames, ages, or jobs were, and they were both satisfied with that. I couldn't lie, the concept of monogamous sex without emotional attachment seemed odd to me, but they were both adults, and they both seemed happy, so who was I to judge?

"Me and my little pet are going to play," Bella told me, clipping her lead onto the man's collar. "Relax, explore, don't do anything you are uncomfortable with." She was walking away and down a corridor, opposite to the way we came in, the man trailing behind her on his leash before it clicked that I was being left completely alone for a while. Shit. I shifted in my seat, looking around me and trying to take everything in, but I felt too much like an intruder, observing things I shouldn't. I focused on the signs on the doors around the room, labelled for each of the seven deadly sins, and I had to admit I was curious about what went on in them. A striking woman with long blonde hair up in a high ponytail, wearing a grey t-shirt with the clubs' logo on, walked out of the room labelled 'Gluttony', leaving the door open behind her. Bella had said I shouldn't look in one when the door was closed, but if it were open already and empty, it wouldn't hurt anyone if I had a quick look around, would it? Curiosity had always been in my nature, so my feet were quickly taking me towards the tempting open door. I had wanted to see the decor, the furniture, and what weird sex toys were lying around, but it wasn't like I had imagined. The walls were painted a deep burgundy accented with a gold band through the middle.

Painting Gluttony

The room was neat and tidy, with sealed cupboards to one side that hid their contents from me, with sofas and weird seats dotted around—it could have been in an old-fashioned yet kinky living room.

Everything faded away from me as my eyes honed in on the most attractive man I had ever seen. His messy hair was a shade of reddish brown, and he was only wearing a pair of worn blue jeans that clung teasingly to his hips, leaving his chiselled chest on full display. He was standing near an easel, looking furious, and my lower body clenched in excitement which left me confused by my reaction. His frown seemed to spur my libido on somehow. Like he sensed he was being watched, his eyes sprang up to meet mine, his dazzling green ones boring into mine, and it was like being struck by lightning.

CHAPTER THREE

Joe

Adjusting the easel and stool so they had the perfect view of the sofa made me sigh in satisfaction. Everything was finally ready for tonight's session, the one that I had been waiting weeks for. Managing to book one of the sin rooms at Seven Deadly Sins had been a chore in itself, and then I needed to find a submissive who was willing to let me Dominate them and then paint them. My work has been displayed in a few big galleries, so they would know that anyone could end up seeing the painting—seeing them captured in that moment of gluttonous pleasure forever wasn't just for my own personal viewing pleasure. I fiddled with my sketching pencils I had set out on a small table next to the easel, my nervousness irritating me. This wasn't my first time being a Dom, but it was hard to find a woman I liked that would also submit to me, so I really needed this to go well.

A gentle knock on the door sent that familiar rush of excitement through me that always arose when I was about to combine two of the things I enjoy the most: painting and dominating a willing submissive. I was slightly disappointed when Chantelle, one of the club's new owners stepped inside rather than Natalie, the sub I was waiting for. Chantelle had only recently bought the club after the previous owner had been found guilty of a series of murders, but I knew her as a Domme here for a few years before that. Some people hadn't liked that Chantelle was keeping this place open after the murders, but I couldn't be more grateful that she had. I needed this place. She was in full working mode tonight, wearing her jeans and a grey t-shirt with the club's logo splashed across the chest.

"Hi Joe, Natalie just called me," her regretful tone told me everything I needed to know.

"She cancelled, didn't she?" I could hear the disappointment in my own voice as I tried to reign in my frustration. I knew Natalie could be flaky, but I had taken a chance on her anyway. I was that desperate.

"Yeah, sorry, hun, do you want me to help you pack up?" she leaned on the door frame, trying to gauge my reaction and see if I wanted a friend to talk to or not.

"No, I'm going to tidy up and be frustrated, but thank you for the offer," I gave her a soft smile, which she returned. She was a beautiful woman, but the fact that she was a fellow Dominant in nature meant I had only ever viewed her as a peer rather than a possible sexual partner. She nodded her head in understanding and left me to my thoughts. I was too angry and hurt from being stood up for company right now.

I was still scowling into space, refusing to move and accept my fate, when another face peeked around the doorway. Her beauty took me by surprise, my brain short-circuiting for a moment as I tried to take her in. I knew most people here, but I had never laid eyes on this long-haired, brunette goddess before. Her eyes drew mine like magnets, rendering me useless for a good few seconds.

Painting Gluttony

"Can I help you?" It came out harsher than I meant, and I cringed when she mumbled a frightened apology and began to retreat. "No! Don't go. Come in," I called, sounding slightly desperate. I was, but I didn't want her to know that. I couldn't let this goddess out of my sight before I knew more about her. It was a sudden and urgent compulsion that I had to obey. She shuffled into the room uncertainly, tucking strands of her chestnut hair behind her ears and looking at the floor. She had an air about her like a child that had been caught doing something they shouldn't, and I ached to punish her over my knee. Her hair reached her waist in soft waves, framing her angelic face and perfect hourglass figure. My dick was already straining against my jeans just at the sight of her, and when she bit her plump bottom lip nervously, I had to suppress a groan at the mental image of those lips wrapped around my cock, trying to take it all in her sensual mouth.

"Why were you looking in here?" I asked as gently as I could, not wanting her to try and bolt again before I had had a chance to tame her.

"I'm sorry, the door was open, and I thought it was empty," she rambled nervously, "and I was just curious."

"It's your first time in a place like this, isn't it?" I realised aloud. Unsure if it was a good thing that I could be her first Dom or a bad thing that I would have to start slowly with her as a new submissive.

"Is it that obvious?" She smiled ruefully and finally looked over at me again. I felt like a deer caught in high-beam headlights as I momentarily lost everything around me but the sight of her sparkling hazel eyes. I gave myself a mental shake. I needed to focus so I didn't screw this up.

"Come in and sit down," I pointed to the stool in front of my easel, putting authority into my tone as I needed to see if she was willing to submit to me. I suppressed a groan as she immediately followed my order and carefully sat down on the stool. Yeah, she was definitely a natural submissive. "I'm Joe," I introduced myself.

"Laurel," she replied with a small, uncomfortable shrug.

"What made you want to come here tonight?" I asked, standing up to close the door, so no one could interrupt whatever was about to happen in here and to make Laurel feel more at ease that this was just between us, like we were in our own private bubble.

"My friend comes here a lot, and she wanted me to loosen up and stop working so much," she smiled softly, her eyes back on the floor.

"You're a workaholic?" she nodded at my question. She definitely had a naturally submissive nature, but I could tell it would need coaxing out of her gently, bit by bit until she learned to embrace it. "Is this somewhere you have fantasies about coming?" Another nod was beautifully set off by a deep blush on her cheeks that had me wondering if her arse cheeks would turn a similar shade when I spanked them, and my palm itched to find out.

"Has anyone ever Dominated you before?" The question made her blush deepen as she shook her head. "I expect you to answer me when I ask you a question," I growled gently, pushing my Dominance on her a little more. Her head shot up, and she looked at me in surprise, her eyes wide. And aroused. Perfect.

"No, they haven't."

"Good girl," the praise from me made her squirm on the stool as she tried to ease the arousal between her legs. All those needy feelings she didn't know how to manage. She didn't need to worry, as I had plans to take care of that very soon. "Now, tell me, is there anything that you wouldn't ever want to try?"

"Well," she shifted uncomfortably now, "the idea of being in real pain or not being able to breathe scares me."

"Good girl, now tells me what arouses you the most," another squirm in her seat. She was responding beautifully.

"I like it when a man takes charge," her quiet voice went straight to my dick with those magic words. Now I needed to see if I could seal the deal.

"Do you want to try being a sub for me right now?" I growled.

CHAPTER FOUR

Laurel

"What?" I managed to stammer out. Surely I couldn't possibly have heard him right, could I? I had been aching for him to touch me, but I hadn't expected him to be interested in me, never mind be such a gentleman and ask me first.

"Do you want to submit to me?" he asked again, an edge of authority in his tone that had my nipples hardening.

"I've never..." I began, wanting to do anything to please the handsome alpha male in front of me, but I couldn't suppress my nerves as to what exactly that would entail. My mouth was suddenly incredibly dry.

"You've already told me that," his gruff tone sent a shiver of anticipation through me. "Do you know the standard safe words?"

"Yes," I was transfixed by his green eyes that studied me with an intensity I had never experienced before, and I was frozen in place, torn between desire and fear.

"Yes?" he barked angrily, sending a flush of heat south.

"Yes, Sir," I answered hesitantly, trying desperately to remember Bella's coaching from earlier. It had seemed silly, her reciting all that information to me, but now I was wracking my brain to remember everything. His pleased smile and nod let me know I had said the right thing, and I found it slightly odd how proud I was about pleasing this intoxicating man.

"I would like to paint you too, if I may?" his question threw me off balance. Bella hadn't prepared me for anything like this. Was this a fetish of his?

"Paint me?" I blurted out, quickly adding a "Sir" at the end when he raised his eyebrows at me expectantly.

"I'm an artist, and after our session I would like to paint how you look after so much gluttonous pleasure," his seductive tone made my lower body clench in excitement for what I could be consenting to—but my brain just couldn't shut out the wave of self-conscious thoughts at being so exposed.

"I don't want anyone to see me," I fold my arms across my chest protectively and shift from foot to foot, expecting him to dismiss me for being silly and wasting his time. His soft, understanding smile surprised me.

"You don't have to do anything you don't want to do," his sweetness makes my underwear even damper, and I inwardly curse him for being so damn irresistible. "I will ask you again later about being painted; I can even just paint your face and keep your beautiful body for my eyes only." His sensual words as his eyes roved my body hungrily had me barely restraining myself from launching off my stool and onto his lap to beg him to touch me. "Shall we begin?" he asked, his eyes boring into mine, like he knew just how excited and needy I was, but he was still seeking my consent before we took this any further.

"Yes, Sir," left my mouth in a hoarse whisper, and a smirk appeared on Joe's face. It's humiliating that he knows how aroused I am, but the feeling of that humiliation just sent my eagerness for him through the roof.

"We will start slowly, don't worry. Now take off the dress," his tone implied there was no room for argument, and I didn't want to either—I ached to comply. I reached for the hem of the little black dress and tugged it over my head in one fluid movement, leaving me in my heels and my matching lacy black underwear under the intense gaze of the handsome man who was ready to Dominate my body and mind.

"Good girl, and exceptionally beautiful," his praise made me beam with pride. "Lie down on the bench, face up." I complied with this order, sitting down and relaxing back onto the oddly shaped bench that reminded me of a weight bench at a gym. I quickly discovered the only way to lie comfortably was with my legs open. My knees draped over either side of the bench, which left me feeling incredibly exposed and made my libido soar. "Do you enjoy having your nipples played with?" the tone in which he asked this question was extremely casual like we were discussing if I liked pasta. I thought about my ex-boyfriend's gropes of my breasts—that had been ok, I guess.

"I think so, Sir." He studied my face as if he could sense my uncertainty.

"Show me what you like," he barked the order, and I froze. I had never done anything like that to myself, never mind with someone watching. Joe must have sensed my hesitation as he added: "I don't like to be kept waiting, and I hate repeating myself." His tone was harsh and unforgiving, and my hands began caressing my nipples through my bra before I even thought about moving them, my yearning to please him taking over. They were both still firmly to attention, so the caresses over the sensitive tips were quite pleasurable.

"Pinch them." His order excited me, and I began to gently tug on my nipples. I was shocked at the pleasure that shot straight to my crotch. "Harder," he growled, and I was all too happy to obey. Breathy moans escaped me; I'd never realised that my breasts could be the source of so much pleasure. This man seemed to know my body even better than I did, and he hadn't even touched me yet.

"Feel how wet you are and describe it to me." The order made my cheeks heat with embarrassment, but his tone let me know it was an order and not a request. I slid one of my hands down my body and under the black lace of my knickers. I could feel how damp they were before I nudged them to the side and stroked one finger through my dripping-wet folds, letting out a soft groan at the sensation.

"I'm soaked, Sir. I've never been this wet without being touched by someone else before," I gasped, my fingers moving of their own accord as I slid one of my fingers deep inside me, needing to do something to try to ease the burning arousal that built inside me.

"Good girl," Joe's praise made me grow even wetter, "now, take that soaked finger you're currently fucking yourself with and move it to your clitoris. Keep pinching and rubbing it until I tell you to stop."

"Yes, Sir," I rushed to obey, desperate for some friction on the little bundle of nerves. I gasped and rocked my hips at the sensation and knew an orgasm would be upon me quickly. I heard Joe stand and shuffle around the room, moving things around that I couldn't see, but I couldn't stop circling my clit even if I had wanted to. My orgasm crashed over me, so much more intense than anything I had ever felt, my legs trembled, and I was bucking my hips wildly. I had been touching myself since I was a teenager, but it had never felt like this before. As I slowly came down from my high, my arms flopped limply over the sides of the bench, pleasantly sated from my orgasm and panting slightly from the exertion.

"I didn't tell you to stop," Joe growled before landing a slap on each of my covered breasts. "For that, you lose underwear privileges. Take it all off now and resume fingering that little bud that drives you wild." My breasts were stinging with the slight pain of the slaps, but this quickly faded to a pleasurable buzz that lit the fire inside me all over again. I practically tore off my bra and kicked my knickers away without even sitting up from the bench, my fingers eager to resume their task. I felt deliciously vulnerable being fully naked, touching myself with my legs spread wide, all-in front of the semi-dressed muscular male dominating me. I shuddered pleasantly at the thought that he was far from done with me.

I felt something large, and silicone pressed into one of my hands as my other hand continued gently tugging on my clit. I tilted my head forward to see that Joe had handed me a huge, firm, purple dildo that he had thoughtfully slathered in some form of lube. I felt my eyes widen in shock. It's huge. Much bigger than anything I've had inside me before, real or fake. Joe was gazing at me, his eyes raking over my pebbled nipples, and my fingers deftly worked over my bundle of nerves as I began to arch my back and moan as his watchful gaze ignited an inferno inside me. To the side, I spotted a table with an array of toys laid out, most of which I didn't have a clue what they did, but I suspected I would find out soon.

"Fuck yourself with the dildo, and the more you get inside you, the better your reward," his voice had taken on a gravelly quality, letting me know he was as affected by this connection between us as I was. I eyed the huge member in my hands slightly nervously before gritting my teeth in determination. I wanted to please Joe, and I really wanted whatever that reward was, so I knew what I had to do.

CHAPTER FIVE

Laurel

Gripping the rigid, purple member, I slid it over my entrance, warming it up a little before I slid it inside me. It started to stretch me with its girth immediately. I only had a few inches inside me when the sensation of being so full and tight made me stop pushing and instead begin slowly pulling the dildo out and then gently back in. The overwhelming sensation of pleasure had me bucking my hips against the dildo already, and I didn't have much of it inside me. I had the sudden urge to know if what I was doing pleased Joe, so I sat up slightly on the bench and found him staring at me with rapt attention, arousal in his eyes, and I could see his hard cock straining against his jeans. Holy shit, it looked like he had a huge piece of pipe stuck down his pants, the outline of his cock going down the leg of his jeans, and I felt myself begin to crave him even more as he looked much bigger than the dildo I was currently struggling with.

"You'll have to do better than that," his gravelly voice made my pussy clench in anticipation, and I really hoped he would replace the plastic cock with his own.

Redoubling my efforts to please Joe, I increased my pace, thrusting the dildo in and out of me, pulling less out and pushing more in, relishing the feeling of being stretched further until I had a good seven or eight inches inside me. Joe was still watching me with his piercing green eyes, and it made me so much wetter I began to emit an embarrassing squelching sound with each thrust.

"Pinch your clit and send yourself over the edge," he growled. And I did. Squealing, squelching and bucking over the edge of the most amazing orgasm I had ever experienced, never losing eye contact with those passionate green orbs gazing down at me. My limbs flopped over the bench in exhaustion as the dildo slipped out of me and fell to the floor with a thunk as I gasped and panted my way back down to planet Earth.

"Colour?" Joe's voice penetrated my haze of pleasure, and it took my scrambled brain a few moments to understand his question. He was checking in to see how I was. I was fucking fantastic. Did I want to carry on? Hell yes!

"Green, Sir," I panted.

"Good girl," he patted my leg, and rather than feeling like the gesture was condescending, I felt proud, like I had earned his praise. "I don't usually reward disobedience, but as this was your first time, let me give you what you deserve."

This time he inserted a vibrator and instantly turned it right up. I jumped at the unexpected, intense vibrations straight on my already sensitive core, shuddering with pleasure and tried to resist the urge to close my legs to calm the intensity. Joe was relentless, thrusting the vibrator in and out of me, the rabbit ears bouncing on and off my clit, making my legs tremble uncontrollably. My hands tangled in my hair to keep from interrupting the powerful sensations cascading over me. I began writhing and moaning as my orgasm crashed over me—it was a heady cocktail of pleasure and pain on my poor overstimulated body.

"Joe! Oh my God! Holy fuck! Stop! It's too much! Yes!" I cried out on a loop, not even caring that everyone outside the room could probably hear me. The pleasure was too great.

"I normally prefer to be called Sir or Master when we are playing," he scolded me, abruptly turning off and removing the dildo, tossing it to the floor. God help me, I whined that the rapture had stopped. "Don't disrespect me again," he growled and roughly pinched my swollen clit which still ached and pulsed from three orgasms in quick succession. The pinch sent another wave of the heady pleasure/pain mixture through me, and I started to get aroused all over again at his rough treatment of my body, causing me to groan loudly. I didn't know if I wanted this Adonis to stop, as the pleasure he gave me was too much, or if I never wanted him to stop.

I watched in silent anticipation as Joe stalked around my sprawled form and stopped by the top of my head. His hands slid under my armpits and slid me further up the bench until my head dangled over the end. I suspected what was coming next when he started to unbutton his jeans slowly and slid them down over his hips. His cock sprang free, and I finally got my first look at it. I'd never seen one so long and thick. There was no way I would fit it all in my mouth, even with his pre-cum dripping off his head teasingly, ready to ease the way.

"Suck my cock," he barked, and his words went straight to my pussy. I wanted his cock filling my mouth, and I hoped as a reward, my abused genitals might get filled by it too. I licked my lips and readied myself, eager to please my Master.

I leant up and gently licked the drop of pre-cum, humming at its deliciously salty taste. I greedily lapped at the head of his cock before I ran my tongue up and down his shaft a few times, earning a soft groan from Joe. Pleased with how I was doing, I stretched my neck and sucked the head into my mouth, my jaw cracking with its girth. A gentle thrust from Joe at this angle had him easily sliding to the back of my throat, triggering my gag reflex a little. I looked at the huge shaft of his cock that wasn't in my mouth and huffed in frustration, as I wasn't even halfway there yet. Joe withdrew a little, and it gave me a chance to breathe through my nose, readying myself for his next thrust. As Joe began a gentle rhythm fucking my mouth, I re-doubled my efforts, trying to suck as much of his cock into my mouth as I could, my gag reflex relaxing slightly. Joe completely withdrew from my mouth with a grunt, stepping back from me. I felt embarrassed that I couldn't please him and looked up at him, begging him with my eyes not to be too harsh with me. That gentle smile appeared again.

"I was getting too close, and I'm not ready to be done with you yet," his growled words sent a wave of warmth and reassurance through me. "Roll over onto your hands and knees," he barked, reverting to his Dominant persona once more. I rolled over as Joe disappeared behind me, my stomach dropping as the bench lowered unexpectedly. I felt his hand start to caress the soft skin of my backside, stroking each cheek in turn, and I was suddenly in a state of aroused high alert for what might come next.

"Your arse is almost perfect, Laurel," he growled as he continued to touch me, making me shudder with the electricity his touch provoked.

"Almost, Sir?" I had to ask.

"All submissives, when playing with their Masters, should have blushing red arse cheeks to remind them of their place." I should have seen it coming, but I still jumped in shock when a handful of spanks rained down on my rear. I braced my hands on the sturdy bench as the mixture of pleasure and pain sent me into a state of euphoria.

"Colour?" came a soothing voice in my ear as he kneaded and soothed my stinging flesh. My head was spinning, and the sharp sting of the spanks had faded to a pleasurable burn that went straight to my core, making me groan rather than answer. A hard spank on each cheek chastised me for not giving him an answer as I slumped down on the bench with a whimper, my arms giving out.

"Green, Sir," I mumbled into the soft leather that was still scorching hot from my skin. Two more hard spanks rained down that made me yelp and writhe.

"Your arse should always be held high for your Master," spank, "your body is mine to do with as I please," spank, spank, "do not disobey me again!" he yelled as I quickly pulled myself up onto all fours, but the harsh spanking continued. I began to yelp with every strike, tears springing to my eyes at the continuous sharp sting, but I kept my arse high and didn't say a word. I had disobeyed and deserved punishment. I needed to please him, and the sweet arousal that dripped down to my knees made it clear I loved every second of the brutal treatment. Finally, the spanks subsided into gentle rubs and caresses of my flaming skin, but my arousal was at boiling point.

"Thank you, Sir," I heard myself cry out, and I really was grateful. I realised I needed this kind of treatment, and I was overwhelmed with affection and gratitude for the man dishing that punishment out. I heard Joe curse under his breath, and suddenly he was in front of my face, tilting my chin up to look at him.

"I know I said we would go slow tonight, but it's taking all my willpower not to fuck you long and hard until you can't walk right tomorrow, and I'm losing. Last chance to call red or amber Laurel, colour?" His eyes looked like they were pleading with me in some weird role reversal, but as I shifted my thighs, desperate for some friction between my legs, we both knew the answer.

"Green!" I cried. "Green, please, Joe, Sir, please!" I was humiliatingly needy but too far gone to care. Joe disappeared behind me again, and the sound of a condom being opened was music to my ears as I waggled my glowing backside impatiently. When I finally felt his cock nudging at my entrance, I began begging all over again, amazed at what was coming out of my own mouth; "please, Sir, please fuck me, Sir, fuck me please!" I babbled. I was usually far too self-conscious during sex to dream of saying anything, but it felt too natural to stop right now. Joe began pushing into me, and I could only throw my head back and moan. Inch after inch slid inside me as he stretched and filled me despite the dildos and my previous orgasms. I felt so full, but more and more cock kept being pushed inside me. Just as the fullness began to get too much, I felt Joe's thighs hit the back of my own, and I groaned with mixed relief and satisfaction.

"Fuck, Laurel!" he cursed from behind me, his hands gripping my hips in a vice. He gently rolled his hips, letting me adjust to his size for a few long seconds before he began withdrawing and plunging back in at a brutal pace. The contrasting feelings of being so tightly stretched and then so tragically empty had me wailing with neediness. Joe upped his pace again as he hammered into me, and he took hold of my hair and used it as reins to hold me in place while he brutally fucked and used my pussy. And holy fuck did it feel good. White lights began to flash in front of my eyes as a pleasure I had never known consumed me, and I screamed and cried out my release, unable to stop my arms from collapsing underneath me.

Joe released my hair and used his strong arms to lift me, so I was upright and leaning back against his bare chest, and both our skins slick with sweat. As he began pounding into me again, I felt an unusual sensation, like I suddenly needed to pee so badly I might burst. That unusual sensation faded, leaving me feeling like something inside me was building with a huge explosive pressure, and each delicious rub of Joe's huge cock on my inner walls took me further and further towards detonation.

"I that my...? I've never..." I rambled in wonder, as Joe kept up his furious pace, pounding my G-spot and enlightening me on more of what I had been missing out on.

"Get used to it. You submit so fucking beautifully. You're mine," his voice was strained, and his pace became erratic as he neared his own completion. The pressure finally burst inside me and flew like a tidal wave over my body, everything fading into perfect bliss.

I don't know how much time I lost, but when I finally returned to planet Earth I was panting heavily, Joe still holding me in his arms, his ragged breathing echoing mine. He gently pulled out of me and lowered me back onto the bench, where I collapsed in an ungraceful heap. I could feel a warm, sticky patch on my belly, but my limbs were too heavy to move, and I was too satisfied to care. Joe appeared at my side, having disposed of the condom and refastened his jeans, scooping me up and into his arms. I spotted a puddle on the bench where I had been as he carried me away.

"Was that me?" I mumbled, tucking my head into his smooth chest in embarrassment, As his chuckle vibrated in my ear. Being wrapped in his strong arms, my own limbs like dead weights after enduring so much pleasure, gave me such an overwhelming sensation of safety and belonging that it scared me slightly. Bella's sub's choices suddenly made sense, I would happily wear a collar and leash if it meant I got to experience tonight again and again, and everyone knew I was Joe's.

"I've never made a woman do that before, so I'm feeling rather smug right now," he softly kissed the top of my head, and I closed my eyes, sighing with pleasure. I had never felt so worshipped and taken care of during sex before, and I had a funny feeling at the back of my mind that this sex god artist had just ruined me for any other man.

CHAPTER SIX

Joe

Carrying Laurel and laying her down onto the comfortable sofa in the room gave me an unfamiliar sense of male pride as I pulled a blanket over her spent and limp form. I had given her the pleasure that had made her orgasm so many times she probably didn't even know her own name right now. My intention was to paint her, but my body wasn't willing to be that far away from hers just yet, so I crawled onto the sofa with her and held her lightly against my chest. As Laurel sighed happily and snuggled in, I knew I was in trouble. I always kept subs at arm's length and away from my heart, and that had been working for me until this goddess walked into the room. In less than two hours, she had me losing control, kissing her head and cuddling. All things I hadn't done for an exceptionally long time and things I had promised not to do again. Aftercare was one thing, but an emotional connection was a whole different one.

"That's nice," Laurel mumbled, and I realised I had been stroking her hair while I was thinking. It felt soft and silky in my fingers, and the smell of her coconut shampoo invaded my nostrils and had my dick stirring again.

"May I paint your face?" I asked, feeling like an arse for ruining her contentment but needing to put some space between us before I made a complete fool of myself.

"Just my face?" I could hear the hesitation in her voice and the quick glance she shot down to her blanket covered form.

"Are you nervous about posing for the painting or that people will see it?" I asked gently, suddenly yearning to understand her uncertainty.

"Both," she tugs the soft, grey blanket tighter around her, like it could protect her, "I know I'm not much to look at…"

"You are joking, right?!" I'm stunned at her low opinion of herself, "You're beautiful! Anyone who tells you otherwise is blind!" I have to reign myself in from shouting these facts at her. A deep blush spreads across her face.

"I have a huge arse..." she begins, and I wave her off.

"You have a gorgeous arse that begs to be spanked and reddens perfectly." Her blush deepens, and her tight grip on the blanket loosens slightly.

"Could you maybe just paint my face first of all?" she asks shyly, avoiding my eyes. I don't know who gave her the idea that she was anything less than a goddess among men, but they needed their head examined.

"Yes, I'll paint your beautiful body next time we play," I hadn't meant to say that out loud, but when I heard her breath catch at the thought of seeing me again, I waited anxiously for her response. Her body tensed for a few seconds before she relaxed and nodded her head. Impulsively I found myself kissing the top of her head again before I eased myself up. The gesture felt too intimate. I never kissed subs; it implied a deeper level of affection than I was willing to give. Strangely though, I couldn't wait to see Laurel underneath me again while I pounded into her, hearing her cry my name in ecstasy. Not 'Sir' or 'Master', but my name. Yeah, I was fucked. Funny thing was, I couldn't seem to care that much.

My pencil flowed across the easel like water, and Laurel's features became clearer and more accurate with every stroke. A comfortable silence had enveloped us as I sketched, and Laurel watched me with fascination dancing in her eyes. I snuck a glance at my watch, surprised that an hour had flown by. Reluctantly, I placed my pencil down and motioned for Laurel to stand.

"I thought you were painting me?" she shot me a confused glance with an edge of hurt.

"I've drawn what I need to. To actually paint you will take hours, so I will probably start working on it tomorrow," I smiled at her softly, the relief clear on her face. "I think it's time to get you dressed and get you a drink."

I knelt in front of her and held her lace black knickers open for her to step into, dragging them slowly up her legs and relishing in the touch of her soft skin. I tugged her underwear into place and looked up at her from my position on the floor. Laurel bit her lip slightly, and I knew she was as aroused as I was all over again. Damn this woman was going to drive me insane. I kept eye contact as I scooped up her bra and rose to my feet, helping her slide her arms through the loops, breaking our eye contact to walk around to her back and fasten the clasp. She stood obediently still while I crossed the room to retrieve her black dress. She watched me carefully as I resumed my position in front of her, tugging the dress down over her head and smoothing it into place to have a few last greedy strokes of her figure.

I walked towards the door, not wanting this to end but knowing it had to. I placed my hand at the base of her spine and guided her out into the main room. We hadn't taken more than three steps before a short blonde wearing a few belts twisted together to make some kind of dress blocked our path.

"I've been worried sick about you!" she shouted at Laurel. I shrunk back slightly, my hand drifting and giving Laurel's a quick squeeze before I retreated back into Gluttony and away from whatever drama her friend had brought with her. As soon as the door closed, I already missed her sweet scent and glowing presence. Yeah, I was really fucked.

CHAPTER SEVEN

Laurel

Letting Joe dress me felt so intimate, his hands brushing my skin as he pulled my clothes back into place, leaving a trail of fire in his wake. His hand had fallen naturally into place at the base of my spine as he guided me back to the main room. Part of me hadn't wanted to move from my little warm and happy bubble wrapped in his arms, but the other part of me needed a bit of breathing space to process everything that had happened in the last couple of hours. Bella appeared in front of us suddenly. "I've been worried sick about you!" she shouted at me. I felt Joe's hand drift from my back to give my hand a gentle squeeze, before he slunk back into Gluttony away from her ire. Bella fixed me with a look as soon as Joe disappeared that clearly said, 'tell me everything right now before I hurt you'.

"So, did you have a good time with your friend?" I ask her, barely able to contain my grin.

"Don't even try avoiding me," she hissed, and grabbed my arm as she dragged me to the nearest sofa and plonked us both down. "Spill," she orders.

"Well, after you left me out here alone; thanks for that, by the way. One of the employees left a door to one of the sin rooms open, and I was curious. You said not to go in if the door was closed, and I assumed with the staff member leaving it open it would be empty. So, I wandered in and found him, and then..." I shrugged with a smirk.

"You got your submissive on?" Bella cackled, and I felt myself flush.

"Pretty much," I couldn't hide the huge grin that broke out across my face.

"That good, huh?" She mused, and I nodded enthusiastically.

"So, how did it feel?" I thought about her question, unsure how to even begin to describe everything I had just felt and experienced. Words like amazing just didn't seem to do the experience justice.

"Wow," was all I could muster. "I didn't know sex could feel that good or that mind blowing," I sigh in contentment, blushing deeper when I remember the specifics of what went on inside Gluttony.

"Did he check in with you often?" Bella asks with a touch of concern.

"Yes, he did, but I was always happy with whatever he was planning," I confirm.

"And did he make sure you were ok afterwards?"

"Yes," I grin, remembering how right it had felt as I had curled up in Joe's arms.

"Damn, you got yourself a little Dom crush," Bella joked and I burst into laughter. I don't know why I am laughing so hard; it wasn't a funny joke, but my emotions were still all over the place. Soon Bella is laughing at me laughing, tears rolled down our cheeks, and we are drew curious stares from those around us, but I genuinely didn't care. I have never felt this free or comfortable in my own skin, and I never want this feeling to end.

Painting Gluttony

Once I finally walk through the door to my flat and heave myself up the stairs with my high heels in my hand, my mind is still wired and running at fifty miles an hour. I've never taken drugs, but I imagine the high is similar to what I am experiencing now. I don't know what to do with myself. It's nearly midnight, so I should really get some sleep, but I know it's impossible right now. Instead, I shower and throw on some sweats, ready to tackle the pile of boxes that I keep skirting around. I had zero organisation in the rush to move, so I had literally just swept things into boxes, something I was paying for now.

I tugged the first one I saw towards me and ripped the packing tape off the top in one satisfying tug. My small collection of paperback romance novels were at the top, so I started gathering them into a pile in the corner where I fully intended to buy a bookcase. My eye catches a pile of photo frames underneath the books, and my whole-body tenses. I lift the rest of the books away gently, like I am scared to disturb the memories that lurk at the bottom of this box. The first image that greets me is one of me standing with two of my old work colleagues on a night out. The three of us had barged into the photo booth, and we were each wearing a ridiculous pair of glasses and striking a pose that would have made Madonna jealous. We look so happy, and I feel a wave of grief overwhelm me as I remember their horrified faces when they found out what I had done. I turn the photo frame face down in the box and close the whole thing up. I'm not ready to start dealing with all those memories again yet. I hide the box in my spare bedroom, so I don't even have to look at it and crash face down onto my bed, suddenly exhausted and eager to escape from my haunting memories.

CHAPTER EIGHT

Joe

I was practically skipping down the street the next morning, and my mood was more positive than it had been in years. Yes, I had an unpleasant task ahead, but nothing could take away how amazing last night had been. Seeing that beautiful woman so aroused and submissive and then watching her be satisfied, over and over again at my whim, was exquisite. Especially the last time when I had felt her writhing and squirting around my dick. I had regretted not getting to taste her sweet nectar and feel her legs shudder around my neck, but we had a tentative agreement to play again, so I was hoping that was sooner rather than later.

First, I needed to get this morning's appointment out of the way as I spotted the office I was looking for.

The office was a small, shabby looking place just off the Rhyl high street, the solicitors name, 'L. Slater' was scrawled across the door and window, along with a phone number and a list of family law services. It wasn't quite what I was expecting for a solicitor's office, but then again, beggars can't be choosers. I stepped inside what must have once been a small shop and could see that the owner had tried to make the best of this place by decorating the walls a pale grey and putting two velvet cream couches out for clients to wait on. There was a desk that looked like it was set up waiting for a receptionist, but sadly no one seemed to work at the bare desk yet. The sofas were tempting to sit on, but I had been in my studio earlier this morning working on my painting of Laurel and didn't want to stain them with paint that was probably clinging to me everywhere. So instead, I chose to scowl at the store-bought, mass-produced artwork gracing the walls. I never understood why people bought it. Art should always make you feel something.

Painting Gluttony

"Sorry to keep you waiting, I'm interviewing for a receptionist soon," came a woman's voice that I knew all too well after last night. "Mr. Hamilton?" I turned slowly to face Laurel and saw her face morph into shock that mirrored my own.

"You're a solicitor?" I said, dumbstruck. She looked beautiful in a pinstripe skirt and cream silk blouse that drew my attention straight to her breasts. I had to take a few calming breaths when I remembered what they looked like bare, heaving and pebbled with arousal.

"Did you stalk me here?" she asked, sounding affronted and crossing her arms over her chest in a way that just enhanced her breasts more.

"No, my last name is Hamilton. I'm here about my divorce," I explained quickly, before she assumed I was some kind of psycho.

"You were married when we did what we did last night?" she screeches. Her hair is tied tight in a formal bun and my fingers itch to take it down and watch it cascade down her back. She had seemed so relaxed last night, but now she is wound as tightly as her hair.

"Separated and in the middle of a divorce, hence why I'm here," I tried to keep my tone calm.

"Well, I can't take your case. It's completely unethical. You need to find another solicitor," she dismissed me, strutting into the back room as her sexy heels clicked on the wooden floorboards as she retreated. Panic went through me as I chased after her.

"I need a solicitor for my divorce," I all but pleaded. Laurel narrowed her eyes suspiciously at me.

"You can go and find another one then, crack open a yellow pages; there are tons," she sassed me, and my hand itched to spank her arse for her disobedience, but I really needed her help.

"I can't do that," I ground out, avoiding her eyes in embarrassment. She sat down behind an antique-looking desk, and I could feel her eyes assessing me like I was under a microscope.

"And why can't you do that?" Laurel asked in a scathing tone. "Is that because you feel you earned some kind of discount last night?" she spat. I buried my annoyance down and resigned myself to the fact that I needed to be honest with her.

"My soon to be ex-wife is a solicitor," I confessed in a rush. "So, all the local solicitors here know her. They are either her friends who want to help her screw me over or they hate her and want to use me as a pawn to hurt her and don't care what happens to me." I couldn't read the expression on her face to tell if she believed me or not.

"That must be difficult," she conceded but still wasn't giving away if I had convinced her to help me or not.

"Look, I don't want anything from her,. All I want is my freedom and my pets. I made this appointment because you are a new solicitor in the area, and I needed someone to help me who didn't have another agenda. I had no idea who you were last night, I promise. I just saw a gorgeous woman walk into my workspace," I hastened to explain myself further. I really didn't have anywhere else I could go to have someone represent me who didn't want to use me for their own gain. Laurel's eyes were studying me intently. I wasn't sure what she was looking for, so I tried to keep my expression as neutral as possible.

"Okay, I'll help you file for divorce," I practically melted into the chair by her desk with relief at her words, forgetting I was still full of paint. "But you need to erase last night from your mind.

It's a huge ethics violation and could cost me my license," she warned me sternly.

"What made you want to set up a practice here in Rhyl?" My abrupt topic change had clearly thrown her off her game as she just stared at me blankly. "It's a small town that used to be a tourist town, but now it's decaying. No one chooses to come here," I explain with a shrug.

"I grew up here," she finally answers after a minute of silence. That seems like a vague answer, and I was about to open my mouth and demand more information when she pointed to the door and indicated it was time for me to leave.

I was more hurt by her rejection than I wanted to admit, and it made the familiar anger of a dominant who had just been disobeyed by his submissive rise in my chest. The temptation to bend her over my knee and spank her backside until it glowed red had me balling my hands into fists.

"You don't want to submit to me again?" I asked in a warning tone. She looked up at me in surprise, her eyes like saucers.

"I can't fuck my clients," she shook her head, but the arousal in her eyes soothed my anger a little.

"Very well, after you conclude my divorce, you can take your punishment for being so disobedient," I growled at Laurel. I watched her wiggle slightly in her chair and guessed her pussy was already soaked for me as she tried to ease the burning arousal she must be feeling. "I promise, Laurel, you will beg me to Dominate you well before then." Her mouth opened and shut a few times, but no sound came out. I had managed to stun my little submissive into silence, and I finally felt I had my Dominance back.

"Here is Abigail and her solicitor's details," I produced a piece of paper from my pocket and placed it carefully on the desk between us. "Call me with what you need me to do, for the divorce or for your pussy." Without any further speech or action, I stood up and walked out of her office. The bell over the front door jingled joyfully as I stepped out into the sunshine. My new little submissive would be on her knees soon, begging me to forgive her and fuck her. I just had to hope her stubbornness didn't out last my own. My phone buzzing in my pocket snapped me out of my thoughts. Natalie.

"Hi, Natalie," I answered, trying to sound normal. A few hours ago, I had been angry and hurt that she had stood me up at

Seven Deadly Sins, then Laurel had walked in, and I had forgotten Natalie even existed.

"Joe, I'm sorry about last night," the slight rasp in her voice that I used to find endearing now grated on me.

"It's alright," I shrugged, not even slightly upset about it anymore.

"It is?" she sounded surprised. I had to admit I was too. "Well, I wondered if we could reschedule?" I contemplated her offer for a moment, but I knew that if I accepted, it could ruin any chance of anything happening with Laurel after my divorce was done. I'd never felt maddening desire like this before and I didn't want to throw that away.

"I'm sorry, Natalie, I need to find someone I can rely on," I explained, walking down the street and pressing the button to end the call. I felt a little guilty at first; maybe she had deserved better, but I shook it off, she had treated me worse than that, and I wasn't willing to risk anything getting between me and Laurel. I wanted to explore our connection, and I wasn't going to risk anything ruining that.

CHAPTER NINE

Laurel

"What is up with you tonight?" Bella laughed as she placed a fresh round of drinks on our table. I snatched up my third glass of wine and took a large gulp.

"Thanks," I mumble. We are sitting in a booth at The Beehive, our local pub, and as it's a weeknight, it's quieter than normal, but there are still quite a few tables full and people loitering around the bar.

"Seriously, I'm worried about you," she drops into the booth next to me, and I finally lift my eyes to meet hers, seeing her concern shining in her eyes.

"I did a stupid thing today," I sigh in defeat. She knows me too well for me to try and hide my inner turmoil. "I took a job that I really shouldn't have, but the person really needed my help,"

"But that's only part of the reason why you did it?" She guessed, and I inwardly cursed her for being able to read me so well.

"Well, I did it because I really needed the money," I admit, looking down at my wine glass. I know if I look at Bella, I will see pity in her eyes, and I just can't deal with that right now.

"You're struggling?" She asks in a voice so quiet I have to strain to hear her over the surrounding noise. I nod, keeping my eyes locked on the pool of condensation around the base of my glass.

"How bad is it?"

"I'm a couple of months away from filing for bankruptcy and moving back in with my parents," I admit, as tears began to prick the corners of my eyes. I had needed this to work out so badly.

"Then get your shit together," she hissed at me fiercely, and I looked up at her in surprise. "You're Laurel fucking Slater, and you take shit from no one!" She tells me earnestly, drawing a few stares from the bar around us and forcing a small smile onto my face. God, I had missed her being in my life.

"Damn straight," I mumble.

Painting Gluttony

"You've never just laid down and taken, anything so why are you starting now?" She demanded as she slapped her palm on the table, startling me and a few people around us. A grin broke out across my face, as I threw my arms around her.

"I love you, you arsehole," I tell her, squeezing her tightly to show my gratitude.

"Love you more, you emo," she tells me, drawing another laugh from my lips. She's renewed my confidence, and I suddenly feel able to take on the world again. Bring it on.

It was the day after Joe had come crashing into my office and thrown my life into another tailspin, and I still hadn't worked up the courage to call his wife's solicitor. Agreeing to help him had been completely unexpected, he had looked so desperate, and my need to help people had overruled the logical part of my brain. Making that promise to help a reality was an entirely different story. I had to call his wife's solicitor and set up a meeting with them. A meeting. With Joe's wife. My stomach squeezed anxiously. What the hell had I gotten myself into now? I sucked in a breath to steady my nerves and I forced myself to dial the number that was scrawled on the piece of paper that Joe had left me.

"Abigail Hamilton's office," came a sultry female voice over the line.

"Oh, um, hi," I stammer, "I'm Laurel Slater. I represent Joseph Hamilton."

"Oh, so he finally found a solicitor for their divorce," the woman drawls, and I can almost hear her eyes rolling down the line.

"Yes, could I please speak to Mrs Hamilton?"

"She's not available right now. Can I take a message?" I half-wondered if I was talking to Abigail and she was just trying to throw me off.

"I would really rather talk to her," I insist.

"She's not available." The woman's reply seemed final, and I let out a small sigh of frustration.

"Okay, then I will leave a message. I wanted to arrange a mediation meeting to try and resolve everything quickly and easily." There, that sounded polite and reasonable.

"And your name was?" She sounded bored with me now, and it riled me up even further.

"Laurel Slater," I repeat through ground teeth.

Painting Gluttony

"I'll pass that on, have a nice day," she tells me insincerely before ending the call. Bitch. I hoped when I got my own receptionist, she was going to be much friendlier towards people on the phone. I groan in frustration as I realise she hadn't even asked for my phone number, so I was probably going to have to call back in a day or two and go through it all again.

I tried to take my mind off things and started scrolling through Facebook, but a memory appeared at the top of my newsfeed. It's a picture of me and Him. I thought I had erased all traces of him from my life, but here he was, staring at me from my phone with that smug smile. My skin crawls as I remember what he did. Then I remember what I did. Shame and guilt crashed over me, and my throat constricted instantly, so I quickly deleted the photo and threw my phone in my desk drawer, trying to put as much distance between me and those memories as I could. My desk phone rang and I picked it up.

"Slater's Solicitor's," I answered as evenly as I could.

"I will meet you at 2pm Monday to discuss the divorce, just the two of us," purred a female voice before hanging up again. I glared at the receiver in my hand, my anger bubbling up and a sense of dread washing over me about Monday. Shit.

CHAPTER TEN

Laurel

Monday morning, after reshuffling the case paperwork on my desk for the fifth time, I searched for something else to nervously fidget with. I am on edge, and I can barely keep myself still, and an anxious sweat is breaking out down my back, making the white blouse stick to my skin uncomfortably. I've been stewing over this meeting all weekend, and that was probably what Abigail had wanted. the bitch. This isn't just a meeting with another solicitor. This is a meeting with another solicitor who happens to be the wife of the man whose divorce I'm handling and who I let dominate me and fuck me up to cloud nine. Joe had threatened that I would beg for him again before his divorce was finalised, and the bastard was right. Barely a week had passed, and I was already debating throwing all the rules out the window for him. The only thing holding me back was the feeling that I was behaving like a lovesick teenager; was I really willing to risk my career over a repeat of a kinky one-night stand? Probably, but my self-reflection was interrupted by the tinkling of the front door opening. Shit. Abigail was here.

I stood quickly, brushing myself down and straightening my clothes, like one speck of dust might tell her I've fucked her husband, before rushing through to the reception area. I'm surprised by who I see wandering around the room with a look of pure disdain on her face. A small brunette woman, so short she must barely hit 5 foot 3" despite her heels, her designer clothes hanging slightly off her skinny frame. Every hair was perfect, her makeup flawless, she could easily have stepped out of a fashion magazine.

"Laurel Slater?" her honeyed voice sounds scathing as her eyes narrow and scrutinise me from head to toe.

"Yes," I answer nervously, shifting from foot to foot under her intense gaze. "And I assume you are Abigail Hamilton?" I offer her my hand to shake. Her lip curls as she looks at my hand like it's covered in diseases, clearly not happy that I've tried to greet her like a professional equal.

"I am Mrs Hamilton, yes," she turns away to continue scrutinising the room, and I let my hand drop back to my side, my cheeks burning with humiliation. "Is this a real solicitors office?" she asks with a grimace, poking one of my Ikea chairs with a finger, like it might bite her.

"Yes," I reply through my teeth, mentally reminding myself that she must be going through a heart-breaking time right now, I can't blame her for being in a bad mood. "Would you like to come through to my office so we can sit and talk?"

"Oh, you do have an office, how charming," her smile strikes me as patronising, but I let it go and lead her into the back, a bad feeling growing in the pit of my stomach. I doubted this case was going to be as easy and straight forwards as it had seemed.

"Can I get you a drink before we start?" I smile politely as I point her towards the leather sofas in the corner of the room, placed facing each other to make it an ideal area for informal meetings.

Painting Gluttony

"Bottled water, glass, not plastic, obviously," Abigail orders, removing her coat and spreading it on the sofa for her to sit on. I resist the urge to roll my eyes at her as I shake my head at her question. I have a water filter but not glass bottled water, as that feels like throwing money away. "Oh, well, never mind then." I pick up the brief notes I made earlier from my desk and seat myself opposite Abigail.

"So, you've been separated for a year and just recently filed for divorce from your husband, Joe?" I ask, just to try and break the ice.

"Joe?" She gives a slightly un-ladylike snort. "He really is slumming it here, isn't he?" She casts another disproving glance around the room.

"Excuse me?" I exclaim, unable to hold myself back. That time she definitely meant to insult me.

"He's your paying client, he should have you addressing him with much more respect than 'Joe'," she sneers. I have the urge to tell her that he actually made me call him 'Sir' while he gave me the best orgasms of my life, but I bite my lip to stop myself. That wouldn't help anything, no matter how much I would enjoy wiping that patronising smile off her face.

"I asked you here today to discuss the possibility of finalising your divorce through mediation rather than needing any formal court intervention," I explained through gritted teeth, determined to get through this. "What reason did you file for divorce?"

"You have met him, right?" Abigail sneered. "He's scruffy, distant and dull. I needed to stay married to him for two years so I could be compensated for my hassle."

"Be compensated?" I asked, my mind going a hundred miles an hour at her derogatory comments.

"Yes, I put up with being married to and supported him financially while he created his so-called masterpieces, so I should get half of those profits too." My mouth opens and closes a few times, but nothing comes out. I'm so shocked by her callous attitude. "Don't be shocked, sweetheart. He guards his wallet like he guards his heart. I'm betting he used some sob story about being a poor artist to get a discount from you, didn't he?" she gives me a condescending look. "His art actually sells for a very high price. He's loaded. Make sure you bill him for everything you can." She shoots another disproving glance at her surroundings. "Then maybe you can get a real law office."

Painting Gluttony

Her bright smile, like she had just given me some important life advice that I should be thanking her for, made me want to smack that smile right off her smug face.

"Could we resolve this through mediation?" I managed to grind out, pining myself to the chair so I didn't rise to the temptation of punching Abigail.

"Sure, we could. I just want what's due to me," that brilliant mocking smile graces her face again and I know I'm not going to like what she thinks is due to her.

"And that is?" I asked through gritted teeth, holding back a resigned sigh.

"Fifty per cent of all Joe's future earnings plus everything we bought together." Her smile widens as she says this, she's being a bitch and loving it.

"Future earnings?" I can't help but blurt out, "do you contribute to his paintings?"

"I like to think of myself as the inspiration behind them." I think of Joe painting me last week, naked and over satisfied after the amazing things he had done to my body. I stamp down the wave of jealousy that comes over me at the thought of Abigail being in that same position, but I couldn't see the prim and proper woman in front of me doing that.

"Were you a model or something for him?" I ask casually, but both my curiosity and jealousy are dying to know.

"Oh God, no!" she laughs, "I don't know where he finds the whores that sit naked for him. They must be so desperate for attention!" She laughs, and my face burns. Is that what I am, a whore? Desperate for attention? I feel humiliated until I remember Joe's strong arms wrapped around me like they were made for me and the fact that he wants to see me again. I can't let an angry ex get to me. Those feelings of safety and worship had meant a lot to me, and I wasn't going to let her cheapen it.

"I'll book in the mediation as soon as possible. Is there anything else I need to know before you go?" My tone is catty, and I am being rude and openly dismissing her, but I need this meeting to be over with. I'm still anxiously sweating and so tense I feel like some of my muscles will start snapping. I also needed to breathe fresh air that wasn't permeated with her floral perfume. I've grossly underestimated the woman in front of me if I thought she would take that from me and leave.

Painting Gluttony

"Well, that blouse doesn't go with that skirt, and you need to change conditioners as your hair is too dry and flat, your eyebrows are at least two weeks late being waxed and cutting out carbs is a great way to lose some of that chunk." Her arms fold over her chest defensively, and she regards me like she knows she is superior to me in every way and is enjoying pointing it out.

"Don't let the door smack your plastic arse on the way out," I snarl as she rises from the sofa, snatching her coat up and stalking towards the door. At the last minute she spins to face me.

"I don't know what you did back in Manchester that made it so you had to run back to Rhyl with your tail between your chubby legs, but you're going to drop Joe's case before I make it my priority to find out," she spat venomously at me, and stomped through my reception and out the door. I follow after her to flick the lock closed, but it gives me no satisfaction. I want to slam the door violently, but I can't afford the repair bill if I broke anything.

Anger and hurt are boiling in my blood as I stumble back to the privacy of my office, and tears start to blur my vision. In five minutes, Abigail poked every sore spot I had in my psyche. I couldn't imagine living with a monster like that, playing constant mind games. How could Joe have married someone like that? Had I completely misjudged him? Thoughts about Abigail finding out about the literal skeleton in my closet from the past bubble through me, but I shake them off. I wasn't backing down to her or dropping Joe's case. He needed someone on his side to get through this, and I was happy for it to be me.

Abigail's threats hounded me throughout the day. I had come home to Rhyl to get away from all that drama, and now here it was to bite me in the arse all over again. When Bella text me about sharing a bottle of wine, it was a welcome distraction, and her knock on the door to my flat was music to my ears.

"You ok?" she asked as soon as she was through the door, "you answered the offer of wine faster and more abruptly than I've ever known you to."

"It's been a rough day," I confessed.

"Want to talk about it?" she asked, and I grimaced with indecision. I wanted to confide in someone, to spill the whole horrible chain of events, but I knew if I did, no one would ever look at me the same way. "Let's get you some wine," she finally prompted when no speech was forthcoming from me. I followed her as she pulled glasses from my kitchen cabinet and steered us towards the small sofa in my living room. The room was pretty sparse, with a few boxes still left to unpack littered around and some gaps for missing furniture I needed to buy. I had been more focused on setting up my office downstairs than moving in up here. Bella poured me a glass, and I took a grateful swig, the sharp taste relaxing me slightly.

"I never really told you why I came back here," I said, keeping my eyes fixed to the floor, "but I had a few personal issues when I was in Manchester."

"Sweetie, I don't mind why you came back. I'm just glad you did!" she smiled at me, and I drew another breath in, readying myself to finally say things aloud. Bella had been so good to me since I moved home. She deserved to know the truth.

"There was this guy," I started hesitantly, and Bella snorted and rolled her eyes before motioning me to continue, "he was a client of mine. I handled his inheritance dispute, and we got to know each other. I thought he was such a great guy that he might be the one, you know?" It sounded pathetic to my own ears, but Bella gave me a nod of encouragement to keep going. "We started seeing each other more and more, but then things started to feel... off. He would show up unexpectedly when I was meeting other clients or meeting up with friends, like he was following me. I saw him a few times walking outside my house," the words started to come faster now as my voice began to break with emotion. "I was so scared. I tried to break things off with him, but he went to my bosses at the firm, and they sacked me..." my bottom lip trembled as tears streamed down my face. I couldn't contain a sob that sprung free, and Bella threw her arms around me.

"It's ok, sweetie. You're home, and you're safe," she soothed me. Emotion overwhelmed me, and sobs began to heave free from my chest, relief at keeping this all bottled up for months, finally coming free. Well, sort of. I could never tell anyone everything. Ever.

Bella must have assumed that the story was over as she stopped hugging me and topped up my wine, getting up to put a chick flick on the TV to comfort me. I couldn't bring myself to start talking again, to tell the rest of the terrible tale, but

unburdening, at least some of it had felt incredibly freeing.
Maybe I really could get my life back on track and move on from
what had happened.

Screw Abigail and her threats to dig up dirt on me. She probably
wouldn't find much on me anyway. I was going to see this
through, and I wasn't going to run away this time.

CHAPTER ELEVEN

Laurel

I couldn't believe I was shuffling self-consciously into Seven Deadly Sins behind Bella again. When she had mentioned she was going and asked if I wanted to come along again, I had nearly bitten her hand off in acceptance. It had been a full two weeks since I had heard anything from Joe, and it was driving me slightly insane. I had been talking to Abigail's solicitor to try and nail down an appointment for the mediation meeting, so I hadn't even had the excuse to call him about his case until yesterday to invite him to a meeting at my office tomorrow. I was glad I had only left a voicemail; if I had spoken to him, who knows what I would have said. I couldn't fathom how I was going to face him in person tomorrow. And God, was I desperate to see him. The way he had taken complete control of me and given me orgasms like I had never felt before. I had tried to recreate them alone a few times these last two weeks, but it just wasn't what my body was craving. I was craving Joe, and nothing else would do.

I had dressed more carefully for tonight's visit, and Bella's eyes nearly popped out of her skull when she saw me take off my huge parka. I wore a white teddy and lace knickers that were just sheer enough to show the shadow of my pubic hair, topped off with stockings, suspenders and a pair of scarily high white shoes. The outfit, paired with my pale skin, loose, wavy hair and scarlet lipstick, made me look like a tease between a slut and an innocent virgin.

"Looking good." Bella whistled, her eyes raking over my body again. "Who have you got the big guns out for?"

"Just hoping to get to sub again," I tried to shrug her off, but she shot me a sceptical look. "Fine, I'm hoping to see Joe again. Happy?" I looked in the mirror to see my face scowling back at me while Bella's had broken into a full-on grin.

"Ecstatic, I've met him in passing, and he seems like a nice guy," she mused, and I gave a non-committal shrug. "Are you just in this for a Dom/sub relationship, or do you want a relationship-relationship?" Bella's blunt question caught me off guard. It was something I hadn't really thought about any further than wanting to be alone with Joe again.

"Just to play again tonight, then maybe a Dom/sub thing if we get along okay. I just don't have time for anything more than that." I tried to smile and be casual to Bella, but I could taste the lie on my tongue in spite of everything I had been through and swearing off relationships forever. I still wanted Joe. She shot me a look that told me she didn't believe me for a second either but didn't push me further. Instead, she tugged me out of the changing room and towards the intimidating double doors, my heart hammering with excitement and anticipation.

I couldn't restrain my eyes from scanning the room for Joe. He had told me I would beg for him before his divorce was finalised, and he was right because here I was, desperate to see him and beg for forgiveness. His copper hair and boyish grin drew my attention like a moth to a flame. He was sitting across the room from me on one of the huge plush sofas, talking animatedly with a beautiful blonde girl who was only wearing a few scraps of red PVC to cover her modesty. Anger bubbled through my veins when Joe placed an affectionate hand on the girl's arm. How dare he? He hadn't even looked away from blondie long enough to realise I was here. I was scowling at him when Bella tugged my hand to get me moving again, and I trailed after her, relying on her to keep me from falling flat on my face as my attention was still solely on Joe.

"If looks could kill," Bella snorted as she settled on a sofa about halfway across the room. I huffed as I threw myself down next to her, bouncing slightly from the impact.

"What do I do now?" I asked her in a quiet voice, feeling pathetic and lost.

"It's not unheard of for Doms to have multiple subs, and depends on what you agreed to at the time," she mused.

"Just that night and the implication we would play again soon," I whined in defeat, knowing Joe wasn't actually doing anything wrong but unable to shake my anger and hurt.

"Well, why don't you show him what he's missing and make him as jealous as you are right now?" Her idea was a good one, but I hadn't given her a key piece of information.

"He's a client at work," I dropped my head into my hands as I mumbled the confession, "and I told him we can't do anything until his case is closed." I hated myself for even saying that to him, especially with how angry and hurt he had looked.

"Whatever happens in Seven Deadly Sins stays here," Bella told me in a sing-song voice, "besides, there is nothing stopping you from putting on a show and making him jealous."

"What did you have in mind?" I could see the devious smirk on my friend's face.

"I have some time to kill before my sub gets here, and there is a free spanking bench over there," Bella's smirk widened as she pointed to the black padded bench sitting vacant between us and Joe.

"We have a very strange friendship," I smiled at her, not sure if she was kidding or not. Her hand shot out and tangled in my hair, using it to tug me to my feet and drag me over to the spanking bench.

My friend's strength surprised me as she hauled me onto the padded bench, using my hair to hold me in place. I felt the soft tickle of the leather riding crop she normally carried running up the inside of my thigh, and I couldn't help but shiver with pleasure. The whole scenario was arousing as hell.

"Tut, tut, you shouldn't be thinking such dirty thoughts in such innocent lingerie," Bella admonishes me in a sultry tone that I had never heard from her. I didn't have time to process anything else as she delivered two swift cracks to each of my arse cheeks with the crop. I jumped at each one, the biting sting so much worse than Joe's hand, and I wiggled to try and ease the pain.

"Do you want me to tell everyone what got you this punishment?" Bella snarls, and God help me, I'm wet.

I heard the whistle of leather through the air before four more cracks rained down on my tender skin. I didn't answer her question, but my hands moved of their own accord to cover my backside from any further assault, the skin there felt like it was on fire.

"Holy fuck. You're disobedient!" Bella laughed as she released my hair. She grasped my hands and pinned them behind my back with one of her own. I heard the sound of leather whistle through the air, but nothing came into contact with my skin.

"That's. My. Sub," the growled voice sent all coherent thoughts out of my mind as my libido fully took control of me. I turned and saw Joe, his terrifying scowl directed at Bella as they both hold the riding crop mid-air. He must have stopped it from hitting me, I realise.

"She isn't collared and wanted to play, so this bitch is mine until I say otherwise," Bella released my hands to fold her arms and glare at Joe, swiping the crop out of his hand too.

I used the opportunity to turn around, causing me to hiss at the sting on my backside so I could watch what was unfolding.

"She's my sub," Joe's tone was calmer, but he shot me a furious look like he knew this was my fault.

"No collar, no ownership." Bella shrugged and turned away from Joe to signify the conversation was over and winked covertly at me.

"I haven't gone that far with her yet, but I own her," the words were for Bella, but they were growled at me, and they sent a shiver of excitement through my body, both scared and turned on by his words. Bella looked between us with a suspicious glare, and I was amazed at her acting skills! I knew collaring a sub was something special by the way the two of them spoke about it, but I had no clue what its significance was.

"Fine, but if she goes around offering herself without a collar again, more people will make the same assumptions," she sighed and stalked off, feigning disappointment, and left me alone with the seething male. Joe's strong hands gripped my shoulders and hoisted me to my feet, and he pulled me so close our noses were almost touching.

"You are mine," he snarled before he claimed my lips in a hard kiss to hammer home his point. I was completely lost to the kiss, forgetting everything around me as his mouth dominated mine. He finally pulled back, and a wave of confusion washed over me, was that how Masters kissed their submissives? It felt more like a jealous boyfriend's kiss to stake his claim, but I couldn't be sure. I was acutely aware that he had never kissed me before, and my excitement spiked higher than ever.

"Who do you belong to?" he demanded. I wasn't really sure what I was agreeing to, but I knew the answer anyway.

"You," my voice just above a whisper, still overwhelmed by what had just unfolded and his firm body pressed against mine. I trusted this man, even though we barely knew each other.

"Good girl. I don't want to see you with another Dom ever again. If you need something, you come to me and only me." It wasn't a question, it was an order, so I nodded my head to agree. His body instantly relaxed against mine, and he shifted me so he was holding me in an affectionate hug. For the first time since Bella had put me on the spanking bench, I realised the girl Joe had been talking to was gone.

"What happened to the girl you were sitting with?"

"You were watching me? Are you jealous?" he pulled back slightly so I could see his smirk and raised eyebrows, amused by me.

"No more than you were," I shot back, and was surprised when Joe let out a genuine laugh.

"Good point. She's another Domme. I was asking if I could paint her sub after their session tonight," he explained, as one of his hands started to gently stroke my side, sending a surge of need through me. "But seen as you messed that up for me, and I have Gluttony booked for the next few hours…" he trailed off as he gently released my body from his hold, apart from one hand which held mine. He used it to tug me towards the privacy of the room, and I was all too happy to comply, my knickers ruined by his hero act.

Painting Gluttony

"By the way, you look fucking sinful in white," he gave me that dimpled smile, and I almost melted on the spot.

CHAPTER TWELVE

Joe

My brain couldn't decide if I should be pleased or furious with my little sub. I was pleased because after waiting here every night for two weeks for Laurel to return she was finally here, but I was also furious because she had been letting someone else Dominate her. She's mine. I squeezed her hand gently to reassure myself she was still with me, still followed me into the room I was already starting to think of as ours. My dick was already fighting against the confines of my jeans with the urge to sink into her warm core once again, but she needed to pay for her disobedience and disrespect. She needed to learn who she belonged to.

"Did you enjoy the riding crop?" My voice came out gravelled, and I chastised myself. I didn't want to scare her. I glanced out of the corner of my eye and saw Laurel, cheeks flushed, nipples erect and looking aroused as hell. Looked like I didn't need to worry about frightening her as she was right here with me on the edge of desperation.

"Yes," came her embarrassed reply as she looked at the floor, and I had to suppress a groan at her instinctively submitting to me, "but not as much as your hand."

"Now, Laurel, why are you here?" I kept my voice even; I needed her to admit what she wanted out loud, and I know the slight humiliation would add to things for her.

"You brought me in here?" she replied innocently.

"Why did you come to this club tonight?" I snarled, seeing Laurel's eyes become blown with desire at my stern tone.

"I wanted to keep exploring being a submissive, Sir," her voice was quiet now, her eyes averted, as she bends the truth, and we both know it.

"Did you mean to seek another Dom? Did I not satisfy you enough when we were together?" I demand with a snarl.

"Yes, Sir, you did," her tone had a frantic edge to it now, and her eyes pleaded with mine.

"So, you were seeking another Dom then?" I accuse her.

"No, Sir!" she cried shrilly, with panic in her eyes.

"So why are you here, Laurel?" I asked, enjoying the red tinge in her cheeks as she squeezed her eyes shut in resignation, knowing I'd backed her into a corner.

"I wanted to see you," she confessed just above a whisper. I was glad her eyes were closed as I couldn't help the beam of relief that split across my face momentarily.

"Good girl," I praised and rewarded her by wrenching her breasts free from the baby doll and roughly pinching them. Laurel gave a yelp, and I wondered if I had hurt her, but she thrust her chest out to me for more. My beautiful, perfect sub, whatever I wanted to do to her body always seemed to be exactly what she needed. "Wait there," I ordered, crossing the room to the small bag of supplies I had brought on the off chance I would see Laurel again. I had taken way too many cold showers after planning what I could do to her next. I rifled through the bag until I finally found what I was looking for.

"Have you ever used these before?" I dangled the two small nipple clamps by the chain linking them.

"N... no, Sir." She looked caught between aroused and scared. I gently attached the first clamp to her right nipple, and Laurel hissed and gasped in pain. I quickly moved to the left nipple, and she yelped as I attached it. I gently massaged around her nipples to help reduce the pain and bring the overwhelming pleasure on faster, she began to mewl and thrust her breasts out to me again, so I tugged the chain between her two nipples, and she whined out the perfect mix of pleasure and pain. Perfect. She was so fucking perfect.

"Now, bend over and keep your hands on your calves," she rushed to obey me, and her gorgeous breasts swayed deliciously, the clamps tugging down more with gravity helping them, earning a deep groan from Laurel. "Don't stand up or let go of your calves until I say you can. Understand?" I barked.

"Yes, Sir!" she agreed, sounding slightly breathless as I moved around behind her. With her bent over in this position, I could see the damp patch ruining her pretty, white underwear. I couldn't help but stroke one finger through that tight, wet inferno as I tugged the offending garment down, where it fell like a flag of surrender around her wrists. I had expected her to wiggle or move, but my little sub held still for me like I had told her to.

I retrieved a small leather paddle from my bag. It would be harsher on Laurels behind than my hand but kinder than the crop she had just experienced. I swung back and gave Laurel a gentle swat on her right cheek, and she gave a startled yelp as she swayed slightly on her heels before righting herself for me. I started raining down swats, harder now as I alternated between each cheek.

Every time the paddle struck those perfect arse cheeks, Laurel propelled slightly forwards, making the chain tug on her nipple clamps. I could see her arousal glistening on her lower lips and all over the top of her thighs. I kept on paddling, and Laurel's moans increased in volume. I wondered if she could come just from this, but today wasn't the day to find out, as my little sub was still in my bad books, her arse cheeks turned a gorgeous shade of cherry red, reminding her who she belonged to.

I couldn't wait anymore. It had been two weeks since I had last dominated Laurel, I needed to claim her as mine, and my restraint was hanging by a thread. I tugged the condom out of my jeans as my hands shook slightly, and I opened the packet and sheathed my dick inside. I nudged at her entrance, and Laurel moaned in anticipation but kept herself bent over and still, submitting to me. Fuck, this woman was going to send me insane. As I slid inside her, I could feel her stretching to accommodate me, and she felt so fucking wet and tight I tried to think of something else to stop myself from blowing my load like a teenager. I started a slow hard thrust that made sure the chain on the nipple clamps would tug deliciously on those little buds. Each thrust elicited a delighted yelp from Laurel as the sensations overwhelmed her, my thighs bumped against her blushing arse.

I could feel myself getting closer and closer to the edge, but Laurel's walls fluttered around my dick, letting me know she was right there with me. Now she would understand the punishment. I quickly pulled out, yanked the condom off and pumped my dick with my fist a few times, and my cum shot out in thick ropes onto Laurel's reddened backside. She whined and wiggled her hips to try and entice me back inside.

"That was nice." I caressed her arse cheeks to a chorus of whines that made me grin. "Let's get you cleaned up." I moved away to fetch a cloth, and Laurel spun to face me, still bent over. "But I didn't finish," she told me in a small voice.

"Only good girls get to orgasm," I explained as I cleaned up the mess I had made on her perfect arse. She let out a moan of frustration and I could feel myself getting hard again already, the urge to fuck her to release rising like a tidal wave. Damn this woman. I gently removed the clamps from her nipples, and she groaned with delight as the blood rushed back to them, making their sensitivity increase tenfold. I wrapped her tempting body in the warm blanket I had brought for her and dropped a tender kiss on the top of her head, inhaling her sweet coconut shampoo mixed with her musky arousal. Her eyes pleaded up at me to satisfy her as I pulled away.

"This is your punishment for disobeying me. You are not to orgasm until I say your punishment is over. If you touch yourself, I will know, and the punishment will be more severe next time," I warned, and I saw Laurel shiver slightly with excitement at my words. I didn't know who this was going to be harder on, me or her.

"What made you finally come back here?" the question slipped past my lips before I could stop it as the urge to break our silence overwhelmed me.

"I needed to see you again," she mumbled.

"You already confessed to that, pet. I mean, what brought you back here specifically tonight."

"Oh," her eyes lit up in understanding, "my friend Bella comes here a lot, she offered to bring me as her guest again, so I accepted."

"You aren't a member here?" She shook her head no, and the penny finally dropped about what had occurred earlier. "That was your friend that was worried about you last time that was using the crop, wasn't it?" The blush spread across her cheeks and down to her chest.

"I just wanted to get your attention," she mumbled, her eyes cast to the ground. I pushed her chin gently upwards, forcing her to look at me.

"You already have all my attention, pet. I was aware of you as soon as you walked through the door like a mild electric shock went through my body at your nearness," I watched as she shivered, her arousal back up to boiling point, "and if you want me to play with you, you just need to behave yourself," I whispered against her lips, testing the limits of my own restraints. I needed to get out of here before I caved. I needed to have the control in this relationship. I gathered my things as Laurel reluctantly righted her clothes to walk out with me.

"See you tomorrow, Laurel," I called as I walked away from her, far from satisfied, "and don't forget your punishment." I didn't need to turn to know she would be blushing profusely again.

CHAPTER THIRTEEN

Laurel

I heard the bell above the front door jingle, letting me know Joe had arrived at my office. My lower body clenched desperately in my already damp underwear, and I suddenly felt anxious, so I smoothed my hair down and brushed dust off my clothes. When Joe had told me last night that I was forbidden to touch myself until he decided my punishment was over and I deserved an orgasm, I had felt a ridiculous combination of outrage and arousal. How dare he drive me to the edge of insanity, leave me unsatisfied and forbid me from seeking any relief. Sleep had eluded me last night as I had tossed and turned in my highly aroused state, discovering I was more desperate to please Joe than I was to please myself.

When his handsome face and tousled, rust-coloured hair rounded the door into my office, I had to fight myself to stay in my chair and not drop to my knees in front of him and beg him for forgiveness. I didn't even care about my own satisfaction in that moment. I just wanted to please my Master. The cocky smirk on his face made me think that he knew exactly how needy I was right now.

"Good, you're looking desperate to please me, showing you can follow orders when you try," his harsh tone had my knickers getting even wetter.

"Please, Joe," the whine flew from my mouth before I could stop it.

"No," he barked, seating on the sofa opposite me. "Business first. Tell me what's going to happen at this meeting." I wanted to slump onto my chair in defeat, but instead I took a deep breath and tried to get my professional shit together.

"It's going to be informal, to try and settle your divorce as amicably as possible," there was still a tremor of need in my voice that I couldn't help. I'd never felt like this before; that I had angered a man, and I would do anything to make him pleased with me again.

"Get on your knees in front of me," he ordered in a grumpy tone. I hadn't realised my body was moving until my knees hit the floor with a soft thump. "Blouse and bra off. Quickly." I practically threw them off and to the side in desperation as he lifted his hips and tugged his jeans and boxers down, allowing his huge hard cock to spring free, showing he wasn't as unaffected as he tried to make out. "Wank me with your breasts while you tell me about this meeting."

I eagerly shuffled forwards on my knees and wrapped my lips around the tips of Joe's cock, tasting his delicious, musky, masculine flavour. I bobbed my head up and down his shaft a couple of times, greedily taking in as much of him as I could, proud of the groan he let out as I did this. I reluctantly released his cock from my mouth and sat back, wrapping my breasts around it instead. I cupped a hand on each breast and began to pump them up and down in a steady rhythm.

"The meeting is to try and decide who gets what from your marriage without any court intervention," I explained whilst keeping my pace steady. "If you want any jointly purchased items from your marital home." I began to pant slightly from the exertion of trying to talk coherently whilst giving a tit wank, "now is the time to speak up."

"I bought everything, including the house, but all I want are my two dogs. Oh, that's good," he groaned as I redoubled my efforts with my breasts, as his cock began to hit my chin, so I gave it a greedy lick every time it did.

"Why do you even need me to negotiate for you?" I asked, genuinely puzzled. Surely any normal woman would bite his hand off to keep everything of value.

"Because Abigail won't let me have them," he growled. Joe suddenly yanked his cock from my breasts and began pumping it hard and fast with his own hand. "But now I'm going to cum all over your needy, disobedient face." His dirty words officially ruined my knickers as hot spurts of his cum splashed onto my face, accompanied by his soft grunts of pleasure. I squeezed my eyes shut so none of it made it into them, but the rest of my face was covered, and some of it dripped down onto my breasts. I felt used, humiliated and more aroused than I had ever been in my life.

"Clean me up," he ordered as he placed the tip of his cock on my lips. I opened my eyes to look up at him as I dutifully licked every last drop off him, feeling the cum on my face start to dry and harden. "You've redeemed yourself like a good girl," he told me warmly, and I couldn't help but beam with pride even though there was still a large dollop of his cum sliding down my cheek as it dried. "Good girls get rewards. Leave your knickers and skirt on the floor here and go and bend over your desk." His instructions had me up in seconds, and fumbling with the zipper on my skirt, I left it discarded behind me with my knickers. I walked across the room wearing only a pair of heels and his semen painted on my face as I bent over my desk to display my bare backside to Joe.

I jumped when I felt Joe's hand begin to caress my arse cheeks, and I whimpered and thrust my arse out to him, begging for more, of what I didn't know or care, just more of anything he would give me. The caressing abruptly stopped before he brought his hand down to harshly spank my upturned cheeks, repeatedly hitting one and then the other. I whined but kept my arse held high for him, just like he had trained me to. The burn on my arse cheeks seemed to go right to my pussy, and I couldn't help but moan. I needed this.

"I've bought you a little present. I was going to give it to you last night, but you didn't deserve it until now," his voice was harsh, reinforcing how displeased he was with me, even though he had stopped spanking me.

I felt something small and cold run over my clit and pussy lips before Joe thrust it inside me for three swift pumps, then withdrew completely, drawing a wanton moan from my throat. The object moved behind me, circling my anus, somewhere no one had ever been. I yelped and tried to stand up, but Joe shoved me roughly back down onto the desk and spanked each of my arse cheeks again, renewing the burning sensation. This was the roughest he had been with me so far, and I was loving every second of it as he wasn't asking for my submission, he was taking it.

"Colour?" He growled.

"Green," I wailed.

"Don't be ungrateful for a present your Master thoughtfully bought for you then," he scolded when I finally held still again. The object was returned to my anus, and Joe began to gently push it inside, aided by my own arousal he had used to lubricate it. As it finally breached my tight rosebud, I couldn't help but emit a yowl at the intrusion, receiving two more harsh spanks for my ungratefulness. Joe began to gently fuck my arse with the object as he pushed it in slightly further with each thrust. The initial pain and discomfort faded as pleasure began to override it. Joe's other hand slipped beneath me and circled my clit at a torturously slow pace that made me buck and whine for release. "Hmmm, I think I just heard the door," he said casually. Panic surged through me as I tried to stand, but Joe used the object in my arse to keep me firmly on the desk. "Wouldn't it be a shame for someone to walk in here and see you naked, my spunk all over your face, arse cheeks red and rosy as I plug your arse, and you cum for me like a good little sub?" The heady combination of him holding me down, the plug still fucking my arse and his dirty words had me screaming through a climax with an intensity that I had never felt before as my legs and arse shuddered through the overwhelming sensation. With one final thrust from Joe, my anus closed around the other end of the plug as it settled deep in my arse.

"Go to the bathroom and clean yourself up but leave that plug right where it is. I'll take it out after the meeting when I know which hole I'm fucking." I must have looked confused as he grinned and added: "If you get me my dogs, I will be fucking your pussy through so many orgasms you pass out. But if you don't, will bend you back over that desk and fuck your arse properly." I shivered in excitement as my whole body became aroused once again. I had always been mildly horrified by the idea of anal sex, but Joe made me want to waggle my arse and beg him for it. I knew I would enjoy anything he did with me.

"Did someone really come in?" I asked him, horrified someone may have just heard me scream in pleasure. My face turned the same colour as my arse in humiliation.

"No," he replied softly, as he wrapped me in a warm, comforting hug, the smell of his arousal made my lower body clench in excitement again. "I just wanted to see how you were with exhibitionism, and clearly, it's something you would like to try," he shrugged with a smug smirk. I felt myself blushing furiously but knew now that I didn't disagree; the thought that someone would walk in and see me is what had sent me over the edge.

"Go and clean up," he gave my tender arse a gentle squeeze as he released me from the hug, pecking my lips softly with his, and I knew that anything sexual was finished for now. I felt a pang of disappointment as I just wanted to stay in his arms, where I felt safe and warm. But that wasn't the type of relationship we had, so I walked obediently towards the bathroom.

Walking to pick my clothes up and go to the bathroom was a vastly different experience with Joe's plug nestled snugly in my arse. Every movement I made caused the plug to shift and gave me an odd sensation that was a cross between uncomfortable and pleasure. When I finally re-joined Joe in my office, I realised I wouldn't be able to sit down properly with the plug still inside me, and his smug smirk as he watched me look around the room for somewhere to perch told me he knew it.

"Here," he opened his arms and indicated for me to sit on his knee. He adjusted my position there and wrapped his arms around me in a warm embrace, one of his hands gently stroking my back. Confusion consumed my mind at these what I defined as relationship-type gestures. Were we in a relationship? Was I just a rebound screw? Did it mean something that this had happened outside SDS? What had felt like an exciting Dom/sub relationship ten minutes ago now had my mind spinning. But I couldn't even focus on that right now, as I needed to make sure we were both as prepared as possible for this mediation meeting.

"What happened between you and your wife?" I asked. Because as well as needing to know professionally, my curiosity had peaked. Neither one of them would share why they were divorcing, not even to accuse each other of anything. It was a really odd scenario to be in. Was Joe a cheater? Did he have some big secret like I did?

"We just didn't love each other anymore," he sighed despondently. There was something that had happened, I could see it on his face, the slight pinch around his mouth, and the anger swirling in his eyes.

"Tell me," I pushed him gently, covering his hand with mine.

"Nothing happened," he snapped angrily. I stared at him with raised eyebrows that said I didn't believe him while he scowled back at me. "What made you move to Rhyl?" he barked out, the abrupt change of topic taking me off guard, and I wondered for a moment if Abigail had gone through with her threat to find out about my past and he had shared that information with Joe.

Painting Gluttony

"We aren't talking about me right now. We are trying to get you out of your marriage," I snarled on the outside, but inside I was crumbling. Had Abigail told him, is that why he was bringing it up? Or was he trying to deflect my attention away from whatever he was hiding?

"What made you move to Rhyl?" he repeated, looking at me pointedly.

"I grew up here. I wanted to be closer to my family." It was a lie, and I think he knew that from the way he looked at me with suspicion written all over his face. "What happened between you and Abigail?" He wasn't my Master right then, and I would push him for answers if I needed to. Our standoff was interrupted by the bell over the front door tinkling. His wife and her solicitor were here. Great.

CHAPTER FOURTEEN

Joe

I could see Laurel nervously fidgeting with her hair and clothes before she went to greet them like she was sure Abigail would know what had just happened in here. She needn't have bothered; Abigail only ever cares about Abigail. As my soon-to-be ex-wife strutted into the room, her nose curled up in disdain, and I took a moment to slowly study her. She was still beautiful and well put together, but she had a cold distance about her that had taken me a long time to see.

My eyes flicked to Laurel, and even through her nerves, her natural beauty, warmth and kindness surrounded her in a glow I wanted to wrap myself in. As my eyes reluctantly switched back to Abigail, I realised she had just caught me staring at Laurel, and she shot me an amused and haughty look. Damnit, I needed to keep my attraction to Laurel a secret, or Abigail would no doubt find a way to use it as a weapon against me later. I suppressed an eye roll as Henry followed Abigail into the small reception area. Of course, Henry was who she would choose to represent her as he was the choice that would piss me off the most.

Henry was nearly a decade older than Abigail; his sandy hair was edging towards grey, and he had severe laugh lines around his eyes that gave him the appearance of a friendly uncle. His designer suit was tailored perfectly to him, despite his slight pot belly from enjoying many other finer things in life. He was probably a nice guy underneath it all, but I had been suspicious he had been fucking Abigail for a couple of years now. I just couldn't prove a damn thing. He always put on a faux-friendly smile for me that grated me and made me even angrier.

"Joe, great to see you again, mate," Henry chortled, extending his hand for me to shake. I wanted to snarl and point out that I wasn't his fucking mate, but I settled for stalking off towards the small meeting room without a word, leaving his hand untouched. The other three trailed into the room behind me, and an awkward silence hung in the air around us.

"Mrs Hamilton, I'm really glad you agreed to mediation," Laurel smiled around the room, but we could all tell it was strained. "Why don't we sit down and get started?" Her warm tone did nothing to melt the frost in the air.

"I'll make it really easy for you, Abby," I ground out, knowing the nickname would raise her hackles as I leaned across the table without taking a seat. "All I want is Ant and Dec. If I get them, you can keep everything else, including the house." Laurel shot me a look of disbelief that I had shown our hand so early, but I just wanted to get this over with, and it wasn't a secret to Abigail that I didn't care about material things.

"No, I need those two. They help me with my… emotional therapy," Abigail replied with a smirk that told us all she was lying through her teeth as she settled herself in one of the chairs. Henry sat next to her, and inched his chair a little closer to her.

"You need emotions in order to have emotional therapy," I couldn't help but rise to her bait.

Painting Gluttony

"Well, when you have a husband that can't rise to the occasion, never mind satisfy you, you need all the therapy you can get," she smiled sweetly at me, her eyes flicked to Laurel and then back to me. Damn, she knew I was attracted to Laurel and was trying to ruin my chances. I knew none of what she had just said was true, and so did Laurel, but I couldn't help but redden from embarrassment at the implication.

"Why don't we start again?" Laurel tried to keep the peace while Henry just sat back and smirked. The arsehole. "Mrs Hamilton, normally divorcees split their assets down the middle..."

"I know standard practice. I'm not an amateur," Abigail spat, "either I get everything, or we will just have to stay married," her spiteful smile was pointed right at me. I could never have pictured when I proposed to her and said 'I do' that we would end up here, bickering like children.

"What benefit does staying married give you?" Laurel asked, getting right to the heart of Abigail's reasoning.

"Because the longer we're married, the more I paint, the more money I have to give her when she does grant me a divorce," I grind out.

"I think we've given Joe and his... friend plenty to think about for now," Henry beamed around the room. "Let's call that a day shall we, Abigail?" He stood and offered her his arm, guiding her back out to the front door as Laurel and I trailed after them in an enraged silence. Laurel followed them to the door, but I stayed in her office, not sure if I would be able to contain my rage at Abigail or Henry if I was in their vicinity any longer. Anger fizzled in my veins, and there was only one thing I could think of that would make me feel better. Laurel.

CHAPTER FIFTEEN

Laurel

I seethed as I stomped back into my office, certain there must have been actual steam coming out of my ears. I kicked my chair with an un-ladylike grunt, but it only gave me a sore toe as it pitifully rolled a foot away on its wheels. I noticed Joe still stood there, a terrifying scowl on his face, and his eyes showed his mind was miles away from this room.

"I'm sorry I let you down," I mumbled, remembering it was more than my own pride that had been trashed in that room. Shock flew across Joe's face, followed quickly by concern as he approached me startlingly fast.

"You were amazing in there," his soothing arms wrapped around me, and I felt myself relax slightly.

"How were you married to her?" I asked on sigh.

"I was stupid and gullible," Joe mumbled whilst peppering kisses along my neck. It was easy in those little moments to forget that we weren't a couple, that he wasn't mine to comfort and be comforted by.

"So, nothing's changed much then," I goaded him to lighten the mood. I felt him smile against the soft skin on my neck as one of his hands slid down my body to grasp one of my still tender arse cheeks, and the movement caused the plug to shift inside me.

"Hmmm, I'm not sure if you should be punished or rewarded," he nipped the flesh at my neck and I gasped in pleasure, and all my anger and embarrassment from the meeting just melted away. As Joe raised his head, I was immediately consumed by his emerald-green eyes as his other hand reached up to tenderly stroke my face before yanked me into a hard kiss. It felt like we both began to pour all our emotions into the kiss as our tongues warred and teeth nipped, both of us becoming lost in the shared passion. When Joe finally released me, I was panting and flushed, the meeting a distant memory.

Painting Gluttony

"Play time begins now," he growled, his eyes bored into me, letting me know it wasn't a request. I could only nod my consent and watch the alpha male smirk on his face spread. "Turn around and brace yourself over your desk," his tone made me shiver with anticipation.

I quickly obeyed and leant over my desk like I had earlier, the wood hard and uncomfortable under my elbows. I heard Joe move around behind me, and he kicked my ankles wider apart, which made my arse go higher as a result. My skirt was roughly yanked up around my waist, and my knickers pushed down to just above my knees. I barely had time to register that fact before the first spank cracked across my arse cheeks, which made me jerk in surprise. The swats began to rain down on my already sensitive cheeks, and the sounds echoed around my small office as the sting morphed into a pleasant burn that made me wetter and wetter.

The spanking stopped abruptly, and Joe began to knead and stroke me to soothe my burning skin. He softly ran one finger from the base of my spine down between my parted arse cheeks, and gave the plug a gentle nudge before he finally reached my swollen centre. Joe hummed in satisfaction at how soaked I was while I wiggled my hips and whined, desperate for more as his finger left me.

The tell-tale crinkle of foil reached me through my needy haze, and my pussy clenched in anticipation for what was coming. Joe's huge cock suddenly pushed its way inside me without much foreplay. I was still pretty tight but oh so wet from my spanking and the plug, which made the slow stretch deliciously pleasurable. I sighed with contentment as Joe's hips finally collided with the backs of my thighs, my womanhood now stuffed to its limit. Joe pulled out slowly, inch by inch, until just the tip remained inside me, and in one hard thrust, his whole cock was back inside me. I threw my head back and moaned at the sensation as I heard Joe groan in pleasure, too.

He started slowly withdrawing to the tip before he hammered himself back inside me again. And again. And again. The slow and hard pace drove me insane with desire. I tried to use my hips to increase the pace, but Joe resumed spanking me repeatedly as a reminder that I should keep still for him.

Abruptly everything stopped.

"Tell me the truth this time. Why did you come back to Rhyl?" his voice was hoarse with need, and my own mind spun. He wanted to talk about this now? My body began to tremble, and I shouted a plea for him to continue, which only earned me another spank.

"I needed to get away from a bad relationship and being fired," I told him, willing to do anything for him to keep using me like an instrument built for him. He seemed to accept the answer this time, and his frantic pace began again. My head shot up in surprise as Joe started to pull the plug out of me. The unusual sensation of it being removed left me gasping and clawing at the desk as nerve endings I didn't know I had begun to fire. The plug was swiftly plunged back in, and I moaned at the sensation of being so full again.

A rhythm had begun to form. When the plug was pulled out of my arse, my pussy was filled to the hilt by Joe's cock, and when my pussy was empty, the plug was thrust all the way back in, filling my arse. My moans got louder and louder as I felt my orgasm begin to build rapidly. My skin was covered in a thin sheen of sweat as my limbs trembled, so close to flying over the edge of nirvana.

"Come," Joe growled in my ear. On command, my body crashed over the edge, spasming and riding out the waves of euphoria.

Both the plug and Joe's cock were withdrawn from me, and even though I had just had one of the best orgasms of my life, I mewled in protest, not ready for him to be finished with me. I was an addict for his gluttonous pleasure. But he wasn't finished with me. I heard the click of a bottle cap, and a few drops of cold liquid hit my anus before his cock started to push on the tight ring of muscles, trying to force itself inside.

"I tried my best!" I cried out without thinking, my hands scrabbling on the desk as I attempted to crawl across it away from the intrusion, "please don't punish me Joe!" Joe froze at my words, his hands tightly gripping my hips to hold me in place, the head of his cock just breaching the tight ring of muscles.

"Colour?" he barked. The arse-fuck had been threatened as a punishment, but the more I thought about it, the more I wanted him to fuck me there, to see if I could take all of his huge cock. I needed him to claim my arse.

"Green," I wailed, and I knew what I was agreeing to. Joe resumed pushing himself inside, and I forced myself to relax my muscles. The plug seemed to have warmed me up as the intrusion didn't hurt beyond a minor sting of being stretched even further. A slow rhythm began, each thrust embedded more and more of him deep inside of me. When Joe finally bottomed out, I let out a groan of pride, my arse felt so incredibly and pleasurably full.

"Good girl," Joe whispered soothingly in my ear as he started to thrust, slow and shallow, as I adapted to the sensations. His moans begun to match mine in volume as his pace picked up speed and force the more I relaxed. The pleasurable sensations overwhelmed me, I had expected this to hurt, but the initial sting had faded quickly and left only mind-blowing pleasure. I felt another orgasm begin to build inside me like a swirling storm, and I took a moment to marvel that I was going to orgasm from having my arse fucked.

"You ready again?" Joe grunted from behind me as he read my body perfectly. His pace became fast and frantic now as his own completion got closer.

"Yes, Sir!" I screamed, as I forced myself back from the edge of orgasm. I needed to know it was ok to feel this much pleasure and to let go of my inhibitions. I had always thought having sex like this was slightly taboo, but the intense pleasure was something I had never dreamed of.

"Come," he grunted, and began to jack-hammer into my arse as one of his hands slipped underneath us to tweak my clit. I let go of my body, and screamed Joe's name over and over as my hips bucked wildly, the white-hot pleasure overwhelmed me and sent me higher and higher.

I came back to reality panting for breath and covered in sweat, slumped over my desk like a ragdoll. Joe gently pulled out of me, and I heard him walk away towards the bathroom, probably to dispose of the condom and clean up, but I was too satisfied and exhausted to move at that moment. I was startled when I felt a warm washcloth soothing and cleaning me from behind.

"I didn't hurt you, did I, Laurel?" Joe asked me, barely above a whisper, as he continued his tender and caring act of cleaning me. "I got too rough towards the end, and I lost control. I'm sorry."

"God, no!" I exclaimed and turned slightly so I could see him, he sounded so guilty and apologetic, but he hadn't done anything wrong. "I loved every second of it. I'm just coming down from so much pleasure. You have nothing to be sorry for." I pushed myself up from my desk to try and reassure him, but my unsteady legs didn't help my case. Joe studied my face intently, then nodded as if he was happy with what he saw there. He resumed cleaning and drying me, and tugged my knickers back up and my skirt back down. It all felt intimate on a level so much higher than the sex we just shared; his touches so tender that my body felt worshipped.

"Do you have any more appointments today?" he asked quietly as he rose to his feet. I shook my head to confirm that I didn't, my face still blushed, but I can't put my finger on why his attention suddenly makes me feel bashful. Accepting my answer, Joe turned and walked towards the front door, and my heart lurched in my chest at the thought of him leaving me so abruptly. But he didn't. Instead, he locked the front door and turned the open sign around to closed.

"You live upstairs, right?" he asked while he stalked back towards me in a predatory way. I could only nod dumbly, confused about what was going on. Without any warning Joe scooped me up over his shoulder so I was looking at his arse upside down and started to carry me up the stairs to my flat. The whole thing was oddly caveman-esque and was such an unexpected turn-on for me that I swallowed down any protests I had about being manhandled and trusted Joe to carry me safely.

As he opened the door into the little hallway of my flat, I felt a wave of self-consciousness overwhelm me. Abigail had told me Joe was loaded, and here I was living in a tiny studio flat like a student. Would he think less of me? When was the last time I ran the hoover around my flat? My waves of doubt quickly dissipated as Joe carried me through the hallway to the living room, shifting me around so he was sitting on my comfy little sofa with me nestled on his lap, fitting perfectly like two puzzle pieces.

He pulled the blanket off the back of the sofa and wrapped it around us, and I couldn't help but snuggle into his chest, feeling so warm and content. I heard Joe give a soft sigh of satisfaction as his body finally relaxed against mine. As my eyes grew heavy and struggled to stay open, I realised that Joe was in my home, cuddling me after amazing sex, and it felt so normal, when it should have felt odd. We were just a casual thing, weren't we? Being honest with myself, I knew the answer was no. I was emotionally attached to the handsome man who currently held me, but we hadn't actually labelled what we were to each other. He was still going through a messy divorce so he wouldn't be looking for anything other than a bit of fun, would he? I sighed, knowing I had no clue as to the etiquette of how to approach your Dominant and ask if your relationship was more than a Dom/sub one. I allowed the thoughts to drift away as sleep eventually won me over. Those were all questions to ask Bella later.

CHAPTER SIXTEEN

Joe

Waking up wrapped in a blanket with Laurel's still sleeping form tucked in against me gave me a moment of bliss like I've never experienced before. I still didn't know why I brought her up here, crossing the invisible line into her personal space, I just had the urge to do it, and it felt right to follow it. I had come here with the intention of maybe blurring the lines between SDS, and our professional relationship, but I had gone so far past that mark. The last person I had sex with outside of SDS had been with Abigail 18 months ago. A shudder ran through me, and I couldn't decide if it was because I was thinking about

Abigail or because I realised how deep I was in this with Laurel and that was slightly terrifying.

She made an adorable little sound as she began to return from dreamland, and then she shifted slightly on my lap, and my dick started to wake up too. Damn, what is it with this woman and what she does to me? I'm always hyper-aware of her and aching to please her, despite supposedly being the Dominant to her submissive. Suddenly those big brown eyes were focused on me like laser beams, and I couldn't think about anything but her.

"Hi," she said sleepily, a slight pink tinge on her cheeks, that God help me, I think is adorable.

"Hi," I replied automatically, grinning like an absolute fucking idiot. She flicked a glance down to the watch on her wrist and practically leapt out of my arms whilst trying to untangle herself from the blanket. It would have been comical if she hadn't looked so panicked.

"We slept for two hours!" she cried, "it's almost six o'clock!"

"Is that bad?" I asked, genuinely puzzled by her rapid mood change. She paused from trying to yank herself free of the blanket to blink at me a few times. The fact that I think all this is cute just shows how far up shit creek I am here.

"Well, no," she admitted, sharing my confused expression.

"So, where's the fire?" I asked as I watched her sleep-fogged brain puzzle through my words, thinking how fucking adorable she looked. Laurel slumped back down next to me on the sofa and laughed softly.

"Sorry, I don't know what my issue was," she blushed and before I knew it, I pulled her into my arms and kissed her forehead. I felt her stiffen for a moment before she relaxed into me. Why was she uncomfortable with me? Was I overstaying my welcome? Was this not what she wanted? Was there actually a way to bring up the conversation labelling your relationship when you're over thirty without sounding like a complete fucking moron?

"You don't have any photographs or art on the walls up here," I blurt out my observation and Laurel turned to stone in my arms.

"Sorry," I hastily apologise.

"It's ok," she told me in a small voice, "I just don't have a lot of good memories to look at."

"Family?" I asked tentatively.

"No," a soft smile broke out on her face, and she relaxed slightly.

"My parents are awesome, and my younger sister is annoying,

but I wouldn't change her for the world. I moved back here to be close to them."

"Family does help heal wounds," I couldn't help but smile myself.

"What are you going to do about Abigail?" she sighed and sounded defeated. Her unhappiness troubled me, as in my mind everything with Abigail had been finished for over a year. The divorce was just me and her officially severing ties on paper too. I was also aware that she was trying to divert my attention away from the topic of her past, and I was willing to let it drop. For now.

"How so?" I asked warily, as this conversation was heading into potentially dangerous waters for me.

"She's trying to take away everything you have, and we can't let her get away with it," Laurel ranted passionately, her eyes blazed with righteous fury.

"I told you, all I want is my dogs and to get the divorce over with as quickly and as easily as possible," I sighed. Laurel just didn't understand how futile it was to fight against Abigail. Freedom from her is all I wanted.

"Are you still in love with her?" Laurel asked quietly. A barking laugh escaped my mouth at that statement.

"No, definitely not, I don't even care about her enough to hate her anymore," I laughed. "I just want to finally be rid of her on every level so I can move on with my life." Laurel stiffened again in my arms, and I had no idea why. "What?"

"Why did you guys break up?" her voice was small and quiet and that really fucking bothered me. Where is my feisty girl? The only time I like her submissive to me is during sex, otherwise, I loved that she liked to take charge and sass me, so what was going on here?

"I already told you, we don't love each other anymore," I tried to say it as gently as possible, but Laurel turned her head and gave me a look that said she can sense that was a lie. "I was young, stupid and thought what I was feeling was love. I thought she loved me," I sighed in defeat. Admitting all this out loud for the first time was hard enough, but the fact that it was with Laurel made it brutal. "But she pretended to be someone she wasn't. The woman I thought I loved never really existed. She wanted possessions, and she wanted to possess me, and when I didn't let her, she wanted to move on to the next sucker while she took me for all I was worth."

"You mean she cheated on you?" her voice sounded surprised, but I was too lost in the dark memories to take much notice.

"Yes. With a solicitor who got her the job she has now. I thought I could make it better, and we could get past it. Then she let slip she was only waiting until she could take everything I had to divorce me. I was so hurt and angry I just walked straight out of our house and left everything there. Today was the first time in twelve months that I've seen Abigail face to face," I felt some of my anger recede when Laurel held my hand in hers.

"I'm sorry she put you through that, but you're almost free and clear of her now," she gave my hands a reassuring squeeze.

"I already am," I tell her, and a small smile made its way onto my face. "I was scared of seeing her today, scared of the power she might still have over me, but when I actually saw her, I just felt pity for her, that she won't allow herself to just be happy," I explained in a rush. "I'm angry about what she did, but I'm able to move on now."

"Why didn't you just tell me all this?" Laurel asked, exasperated, and I wondered if I had annoyed her somehow.

"I was embarrassed. I thought that I was the problem, that I couldn't satisfy and make her happy," I groaned mentally at my pathetic-ness, "It's only recently I've realised that might not be true," I gave Laurel a meaningful look, trying to convey what I'm not brave enough to admit out loud.

"I know how that feels you know," Laurel started, and my eyebrows reached my hairline, "to feel that you're not good enough for someone, that you don't meet their standards." There was a dull look in her eyes, and I had the immediate urge to strangle whoever put it there.

"What did they do?" I managed to grind out.

"Pressuring me into what to wear and what opinions I should have, telling me I'm always wrong. He even used to follow me as he was sure I was cheating on him..." An idea came to her that made a devious smile cross her face, and seeing Laurel back to herself again made my heart beat faster in excitement. "If we can prove Abigail cheated on you, we can stop her from taking anything from you." I wasn't sure if Laurel misunderstood the silent message about wanting to move on with her or if she was just too focused on Abigail to really hear anything I was saying.

"We can't, I just want to focus on moving forwards with my life," I held her chin gently, so she had to look into my eyes, and her eyes widened in surprise at what she saw there. Now she was beginning to understand. Finally.

"Oh," she said, stunned. I needed to prove to her that even though I'm not brave enough to say the words out loud, I wanted her as some kind of permanent fixture in my future; even if I wasn't sure what that was, I knew I wanted Laurel in it. I realised I had only kissed my perfect woman twice before, something I had only done in moments of pure Dominant possessiveness, so I lifted her chin and met her lips with mine to claim her in a bruising kiss.

She responded to me beautifully, allowing me to Dominate her mouth in the same way she allowed me to Dominate her body. The softness of her lips and the sigh that escaped as I kissed her sent a soothing wave through my soul. Kissing her was addictive, like a drug, and if my dick weren't aching against my jeans, I could have sat there kissing her into oblivion all night like a teenager. I grabbed a fistful of her silky hair and used it to guide her onto my lap. Even if I was trying to convey my feelings with actions, I still had the underlying urge to be in control. The soft moan from Laurel let me know she was all too happy to comply. I began to trail gentle kisses down the side of Laurel's neck, using my grip on her hair to hold her neck taught for me. She writhed in my lap, and it felt so fucking good. I tugged her top over her head and reached around her back to undo her bra. It took all of my self-restraint not to rip the clothes from her body. Finally, her hard, pink nipples were on display to me. I yanked her hair and neck back again, so the two pebbled tips were right at my eye level and began to greedily devour first one and then the other, giving each one a few gentle nips with my teeth that left Laurel panting and squirming on my lap.

"Stand up," I ordered, releasing my grip on her completely. I watched her stand on slightly shaky legs, her hair mussed, and her eyes blown with lust, and I felt my dick get even harder. I quickly removed my t-shirt and threw it across the room, enjoying the way Laurel's eyes roved my newly exposed skin. "Clothes off," I ordered, my voice hoarse with arousal, and I lifted my hips and made quick work getting rid of my pants and boxers. Laurel's eyes homed in on my dick once she was finally naked, and she started to lower herself to her knees in front of me. I tugged her hand and pulled her back to sit next to me on the sofa, a look of confusion crossed her face at me stopping her.

I heard her sharp intake of breath as I dropped to my knees in front of her instead, I hooked her knees over my shoulders so her beautiful pussy was fully on display to me. She was completely bare around her lips, not a hair in sight, so I could see every detail of her and the glistening of her arousal. Leaning forward, I teased my tongue along her folds, and tasted her for the very first time. So sweet. Like honey. Laurel gave a strangled moan above me as I began to devour her like a man starved. I think she was confused by the turn of events, but I've gotten her too aroused for her to care too much.

I alternated between driving my tongue as deep as I could inside her and sucking and nibbling on her clit. Laurel's fingers glided into my hair as she bucked, writhed, and moaned under my tongue. Every time I felt her give that tell-tale quiver that she was close to her orgasm, I slowed down, wanting to draw this out for as long as I could, to take her to a new level of pleasure. "Joe! Please!" Laurel cried, and my ego preened at being able to please her like this.

"What do you want, my little submissive?" I asked, and dropped a tender kiss onto her clit after the last word. She surprised me then as she pushed my head away and reached down to pull me up by my dick. I should put her back in her place and discipline her, but when I felt the slick heat of her pussy rub across the head of my dick, I was lost, my eyes rolled back as I groaned. "Fuck me, I can't wait any longer," she begged, her striking eyes bored into mine, ordering me, not asking me. With our roles reversed, I pushed inside her before I could think, helpless to ignore her pleas when I needed to be inside her just as badly. I had never taken a woman bare before, not even Abigail, but the feel of being surrounded by Laurel's hot, wet pussy without anything between us nearly drove me over the edge right then and there.

Laurel's legs wrapped around my waist, and I started to piston my hips, so my dick drove roughly in and out of her, setting the pace hard and fast. From this angle, I could see every expression of lust and pleasure that graced her face as our eyes stayed locked together in this unexpected moment of intimacy. Laurel's eyes rolled shut, and I could feel every one of her internal muscles spasm around me as she cried out her release, my vision whiting out as I followed her over the edge with my last few shaky thrusts.

I was panting heavily as I pulled Laurel in for another affectionate kiss. I leaned back slightly as I held her tenderly in my arms and was buried deep inside her as I start to soften.

There was curiosity in Laurels eyes, but she didn't say anything as I lifted us both upright and carried her towards the open bathroom door. A hot shower was desperately needed after our third round of the day, and I wasn't willing to be apart from her for anything right now.

CHAPTER SEVENTEEN

Laurel

The hot water pelted against my body and both relaxed and refreshed me. It had taken me completely by surprise when Joe had plucked the shampoo bottle out of my hands. He had poured some into his hands and started to knead it into my long hair, taking care not to tug on it and gently massaging my scalp in the process. Plucking the shower head off the wall he had rinsed my hair clean before replacing it.

I reached for the shower gel, only to have my hand batted away like a naughty child. Joe repeated this process with my body, gently scrubbing and massaging me from head to toe before rinsing me clean. The entire process had left me feeling relaxed and boneless, the mentally and physically draining day had caught up to me, and resulted in a huge yawn escaping me. "Am I keeping you awake?" Joe murmured against my lips. I couldn't help the goofy smile that spread across my face as I nodded. The shower was turned off, and I gave a small whine at the loss of warmth before Joe had enveloped me in a huge fluffy towel and lifted me out of the shower. My head rested against his still damp chest, and it felt like it was slotting into a groove that was made just for me while his heartbeat was a soothing beat under my ear. The world started to fade away as I cuddled deeper into his warm chest, vaguely aware of being carried into my bedroom.

I woke with a jolt, and sat upright in bed while I scanned my surroundings frantically for the source of what had roused me from sleep. My blurry eyes had rested on Joe across the room, and he had his jeans back on but unfastened, which left a tempting amount of his bare chest and hips on show. His hair was ruffled, and he looked sheepishly at me. The rest of my body had started to wake up, and my desire for Joe awoke right along with it, despite the slight tenderness I was experiencing from yesterday.

"Sorry, I need to get to a meeting with my agent," he explained, pulling his t-shirt over his head and slightly ruining my view. "I was trying not to wake you up, so naturally decided to drop kick your drawers," he shot an accusing scowl at the offending furniture.

"My drawers caught you trying to run out on me, so they were defending my honour," I said sleepily as I relaxed back onto the pillows until Joe threw himself on top of me on the bed, his face was above mine, so we were nose to nose.

"I was going to leave you a note asking if you wanted to see me tonight."

"At SDS?" I asked, needing to be sure if he was asking me to play or on an actual date. He nodded his head and pecked me on the lips, and gathered his things. I couldn't help but feel that he felt disappointed in me somehow, but I had no idea what had just happened other than me being disappointed by our lack of a romantic relationship.

Painting Gluttony

After he was gone, I rolled over and grabbed my phone; I needed to talk to my resident expert in this new path that I was following. The phone rang several times before Bella's annoyed and tired voice came on the line.

"If you're not dying already, you're going to be," she snarled.

"Not a morning person?" I asked, overly perky.

"I hate you," she whined, making me giggle, which reminded me of us being teenagers and having phone conversations just like this.

"I miss your ugly face," I told her as I grinned at the nostalgia and heard Bella chuckle down the phone.

"What reason made you wake me up before 9 am on a Saturday?"

"I wanted to ask you more about Dom/sub relationships," I felt myself blushing and was glad Bella couldn't see me, she would have teased me mercilessly.

"Ooo, things getting serious with Mr. Don't-crop-my-sub?" She asked excitedly.

"I don't know, that's my problem," I sighed. "How do you know if that's what you both want? And how can you bring it up without destroying the entire relationship?"

"Wow, that's some intense questions for me to answer pre-coffee, but I will try," I felt a little guilty that I woke her, but I was desperate for answers. "It's a tough question, because relationships do change, so you really need to talk to him about it and come to an agreement so neither of you gets hurt." She sounded so wise, but I had one more burning question on my mind.

"He mentioned collaring me the other night. What does that mean?" I heard Bella's sharp intake of breath.

"I forgot he said that!" she exclaimed, and her speech had sped up to match her excitement level, "that's a big deal in Dom/sub circles." I pulled in a deep breath, working up to ask the question I wasn't sure I wanted to know the answer to: "Why?"

"It's a gesture of how much you mean to him as a submissive. It means he wants you to belong to him and only him. It's a symbol of you committing to be his submissive for the long term. Did he give you a collar?" she asked excitedly.

"No," my voice had sounded hollow and disappointed. "I think he just said that so you would stop using your crop on me," I gave a laugh that came out sounding scathing.

"Something like that isn't just thrown around, especially not in SDS, it's as serious as a marriage, but just give it some time and talk to him about it if you can't wait." My own self confidence issues had meant that Bella's words didn't make me feel any better or even really register. I always waited for the other shoe to drop with Joe and couldn't help my gloomy outlook. Another idea had struck me of how I could help move things along. "Thanks Bella, you've been a huge help. Sorry for waking you! Bye!" I told her, and hung up the phone to her spluttered reply.

The little tea shop had seemed like a good idea an hour ago, a neutral location where if I needed to run and hide in embarrassment afterwards, I could easily do so. Now I saw that it was actually quite cutesy inside, and I didn't want this guy to think it was a date. I needed his help, just not that kind of help. His floppy brown hair had been the first thing I saw, and he didn't style it any differently today than he did ten years ago. His kind smile and broad physique was also just as I remembered it too.

Erin Coal

"Hayden, thanks for meeting with me," I jumped out of my chair to greet him, and my nerves had got the better of me as I wiped my sweat-soaked palms on my work skirt.

"Laurel, good to see you," he replied, then we had a moment of complete awkwardness where neither of us knew what to say and if we should shake hands or hug.

"Sit down. Let's get you a drink," I signalled for the waitress to bring two more teas. "So, how are things?" I asked as I tried to break the tension. Hayden looked at me with one eyebrow raised at my choice of conversation.

"Things are actually going really well for me, for the first time in a long time," he tried to hide the soft smile that wanted to cross his face, but I caught it.

"Okay, who is she and how long have you been together?" I asked with a grin. "I know your 'I'm love's bitch' smile, so I need details," I explained when he shot me a questioning look.

"Her name is Amy, and it's been six months," he smiled down at his tea bashfully. "She's a writer and just moved in with me a few weeks ago."

"That's amazing, Hayden! I am so happy for you!" I gushed.

Painting Gluttony

"I'm still a little puzzled about why I'm here," he said uncertainly. "You said you needed help?"

"I need some help with something, and it's a little embarrassing," I kept my eyes glued to the table and prayed that the two old ladies on the next table next to us wouldn't hear the embarrassing tale I was about to tell my old school friend. Part of me didn't want to break the happy mood and ask for a favour, but with Abigail's threat to expose me hanging over my head, I needed her out of my life before she could take action, and that meant I needed some evidence against Abigail so she would divorce Joe. So, I plucked up my courage, drew in a deep breath and started telling Hayden my tale.

CHAPTER EIGHTEEN

Laurel

If you had told me a month ago that I would be walking into a
BDSM club with a man who was Dominating my body and mind
to meet a policeman I went to school with, who was now
investigating the Dominating man's wife; I think I might have
erupted into hysterical laughter. Yet, there I was, Joe's hand on
the small of my back as he guided me through the doors, warm
and reassuring. As we approach the table that Hayden Whittaker
and his girlfriend were sitting at, cuddled together as they
watched the world around them, I felt a pang of envy at the

closeness of their relationship and their obvious contentment with each other.

Hayden and I had been friends in high school, and I had heard he had joined the police force as soon as his exams finished. When I finally tracked him down on social media, I was glad I had heard right. When we had met earlier today, and the whole embarrassing story had come out, it had been mortifying. For about a minute. Until Hayden explained his girlfriend was a famous erotica writer and he also frequented Seven Deadly Sins. After hearing the details of Joe's case, Hayden had wanted to look into it right away. Although uneasy about asking for help, Joe had seemed to accept my idea to reach out to Hayden fairly calmly.

"Hi Hayden, thanks for doing this," I smiled at my old high school friend. He'd obviously matured since then, but it had done him a world of good, making him look even more handsome.

"Hi, Laurel, how are you?" he asked before he had laughed at himself. "Sorry, that's a silly question to ask when we are meeting like this. This is my girlfriend, Amy," he introduced the beautiful blonde woman still tucked securely at his side, who smiled shyly at us.

"Did you manage to find anything out?" I tried not to sound rude, but I was desperate to cut through the niceties and get to the point. If I ever wanted to find out what was going on between me and Joe, I needed his divorce finalised and his wife and her threats to expose me out of the picture.

"I did," Hayden's smile grew, "there was some suspicious activity on Abigail's bank account, so fraud is looking into that and my colleague, Sophie, has a warrant for Abigail's phone that she should be hacking into anytime now."

"I thought you were just looking for something to help us get Joe out of this marriage?" All this talk of warrants and hacking had my anxiety spiked. The last thing I wanted was for Joe to get in any kind of trouble.

"With the stuff we found, she's going to be in prison for a good few years too," Hayden grinned, and I practically sagged with relief. It wasn't over, but we were a damn site closer now with that revelation.

"What do we do now?" Joe asked. His face showed how uncomfortable he was asking for help with Abigail, and I couldn't tell how the thought of Abigail in prison was affecting him. I had felt a stab of jealousy as I wondered if he would miss or visit her inside.

"We wait for Sophie to appear here with news and hopefully evidence later tonight. In the meantime, I have a date with my girl," he stood and tugged Amy up and over his shoulder, and he carried her giggling and blushing form towards the private rooms in the back.

"I could do with doing something to burn off all this nervous energy, too," Joe raised his eyebrows at me suggestively, "shall we?" he offered me his hand with a wink, and I couldn't take hold of it quickly enough. I had secretly hoped that while we were here, I would get to submit to Joe again. I couldn't hide my surprise when he led me to the door of Gluttony.

"We're going in there? I thought these had to be booked?" Joe's face broke into a grin at my words, and I realised that he had already planned this, so I grinned back like an idiot while he guided me inside and shut the door.

"Strip," Joe barked, and I felt myself shiver in anticipation as I hastily shed my clothes and left them in a neat pile by the door, and I met him in the middle of the room, completely nude. He started to circle me like a hunter stalking his prey, and the fact

that he was still fully dressed made me feel even more
vulnerable.

"Beautiful woman, what am I going to do with you?" Joe tutted
as he walked around me, which caused my nipples to pebble
and my pussy to clench. One of Joe's hands shot up, and gave
my nipple a rough tweak. "I expect an answer when I ask you a
question," he growled into my ear, his breath tickled my skin.

"Whatever you want to, Joe," I reply, practically vibrating on the
spot with excitement.

"Good girl," Joe hummed, "pinch your nipples." I comply as I
tweak the tight buds harshly in the way I had only just
discovered I liked, but I just couldn't get the same reaction from
myself that Joe could draw out of me. My hands were batted
out of the way when Joe produced the chained nipple clamps
from his pocket and imprisoned my already sensitive nipples. I
couldn't help my sharp intake of breath at the slight pain they
caused before it turned into a burning pleasure. A gentle tug to
the chain had me letting out a breathy moan.

"Hold tightly onto these," Joe pointed to two thick black ropes
suspended from the ceiling. I wrapped my hands around them,

and Joe wound the rope around my forearms a few times so I was firmly suspended. But he wasn't finished yet.

"I'm going to tie your legs too, so use the ropes on your arms to keep yourself up," he instructed me sternly. I didn't know what I expected to happen, but it wasn't one leg being yanked to the side and attached to a shackle on the ground. It had looked menacing, but I was surprised to find out that it was lined with plush velvet that felt comforting against my skin.

While I was marvelling at that, Joe had moved around to my other leg and pulled it even wider, knocking me off balance slightly until I remembered his instruction to use the ropes on my arms to keep myself up. I swayed slightly but felt oddly secure. I let out a gentle groan as I imagined what I must look like to Joe: leaning over with my legs spread wide, restrained and offering my naked body for him to do with as he pleased.

"Colour?" Joe's voice broke through my thoughts.

"Green," I managed to stutter out as I trembled slightly with desire.

"Good, I wanted to reward your good behaviour." I watched him take something out of his bag of tricks and plug it into the wall. It looked like a huge microphone, and as he stalked back towards me with it, images of its possible functions flooded my mind. "Have you ever used a wand before?" he growled into my ear, and the sensation had made me shiver.

I temporarily forgot myself and shook my head no. Joe's face morphed into a scowl, and he shot behind me, delivering six swift spanks, three to each cheek. The unexpected pain made me yelp before arousal flooded me as I wiggled my arse for more. But I needed to be good for rewards.

"No, I don't even know what one is," I obliged him by answering aloud. He chuckled, still standing behind me. A loud buzzing filled the room, and then the wand was placed lightly onto my clit. White hot pleasure soared through me as I climaxed. My limbs shook with the urge to claw at anything or flail, but my restraints held me in place. I could only stay put and take what my Master gave me. Finally, Joe moved the wand away, and left me panting and twitching.

"Wow," escaped my lips before I even made the conscious decision to speak.

"Oh sweetheart," Joe chuckled, his breath tickled my ear, "that was the lowest setting, and I'm far from done with you yet." I groaned in excited anticipation. God, I never wanted my time with this man to end.

By the time Joe was finished with me, I was sweating and limp, curled up on his lap and basking in my exhaustion from all the pleasure he had wrung out of me. One of his hands was wrapped tightly around my waist like he was scared I'd run away if he didn't keep hold of me, while the other traced patterns across my thigh that my orgasm-addled brain couldn't keep track of.

"We should go back out there and see if your friends found anything," Joe mumbled into my shoulder before he dropped a few gentle kisses onto my bare skin that made me shiver.

"If we have to," I mumbled back, just wanting to stay in this little bubble Joe and I had created for as long as possible.

"Is it wrong that I feel this is a little too much?" Joe asked me, sounding uncomfortable all of a sudden. "I wanted my freedom from her, but getting her arrested and sent down just feels like…overkill," he mused. I felt a tug in my brain, urging me to tell Joe everything, to lay all my cards on the table, but the knot of fear in my stomach made me hold my tongue. I wanted him to know everything, but I didn't want to lose him, so I chose the selfish option and kept my mouth closed.

"If she hadn't done anything illegal, this wouldn't be happening," I gave his arm what I hoped was a reassuring squeeze and forced myself to my feet. "Let's go hear what they found."

CHAPTER NINETEEN

Joe

I felt a strange sense of contentment as I sat on the plush sofa in the main room with Laurel wrapped securely in my arms. I'd had plenty of sex and dominated before, but no one had ever made me want to take care of them or hold them like this. Her breathing was steady, but I knew she wasn't sleeping as her hand drew gentle circles on my leg.

"Laurel? Joe?" I recognised the policeman we had met with earlier, and Laurel launched herself out of my lap to greet him. I felt a stab on envy as I wondered if Laurel and this detective had ever been together romantically.

"Did you find anything? Is it over?" Laurel fired out the questions rapidly, which I was grateful for as I was too anxious to open my mouth.

"This is my colleague, Sophie," the floppy haired detective moved to the side to reveal a short, blonde, lithe looking woman. Her hair was tied neatly at the nape of her neck, and her formal trousers and buttoned up shirt told me she had never been here before, as did her wide eyes that darted around the room as she tried not to stare at anyone too long.

"Thanks for helping us, Sophie," I said gently, worried I would terrify the poor woman. She jumped like she had been stung at my voice before drawing in a deep breath that seemed to give her courage.

"Sorry about that. Nice to meet you, even if it is a little... odd," she finished with an uncomfortable smile. Laurel gave her a strained smile in return to convey her impatience for Sophie to share her news. "Abigail's phone had records of calls between her and the accountant that made all the transfers. There is some more in there that the tech team are trying to pry out, but it was enough for us to petition a warrant for Abigail's arrest," Sophie grinned.

"So, it's over? She's going to prison?" Laurel's voice cracked with relief.

"As soon as the judge grants the warrant, we are heading over to Abigail's." Everything I had repressed came bubbling to the surface at once. I was so fucking angry at Abigail. She had used me, tricked me and was trying to take away everything I loved. Everyone had tried to point it out to me, but I hadn't been able to accept that Abigail was like that. That she was capable of doing that to me. Until now.

"I need to get some air," I mumbled and stormed towards the door without waiting for any of their reactions. "I'll call you tomorrow, Laurel." Questions spun through my mind, and I needed to know the answers before it was too late.

Driving to my old home was difficult as my hands shook on the steering wheel with the rage that boiled in my veins. The tires screeched as I braked harshly outside the front door. I expected that Abigail had changed the locks so I couldn't get in, but nothing was stopping me from finding out the truth tonight. One hard kick and the plastic front door gave in, and my leg rang like a bell at the impact, pain striking me like a lightning bolt, but I ignored it and pushed forwards into the house.

Abigail was sat poised, with a cup halfway to her mouth and raised her eyebrows at me questioningly. That only fuelled the fires of my rage.

"Why?" I barely recognised the angry voice as my own. Abigail rolled her eyes at me patronisingly and took a sip of her drink.

"You know the neighbours will have called the police by now," she told me calmly, as she set the drink down and folded her arms across her chest.

"The police are coming for you anyway," I spat, and she sat up straighter then, a look of panic flitted across her face. "Now, tell me why."

"Why what?" she snarled as she stood up and hurried out of the room, headed deeper into the house. I chased after her, confused, as Abigail didn't hurry anywhere. I found her opening a small safe that had been hidden behind one of our huge wedding pictures. I hadn't even known the safe was there. Hell, I'd thought it was sweet she had wanted a permanent reminder of our wedding day on the wall.

"Why did you do this to me?" I hated how vulnerable I felt asking that, but I needed to know.

"Because it was easy," she laughed callously as she threw things from the safe into a bag. I didn't know or care what she took from me this time.

"Did you ever feel anything for me?" The question made Abigail pause, and she finally looked at me.

"I liked you, but no, I didn't love you." Even though she had attempted to say the words kindly, it still felt like she had sucker punched my heart. Everything that every other person had said about Abigail was true. She had used me. She was cruel, and I had been an idiot.

"Sign the divorce papers," I growled as the idea struck me. Abigail looked stunned and I took a little sadistic pleasure from that. "I know you have them somewhere here, so sign them, and I'll let you leave, don't, and I'll carry you down to the police station myself," my own voice sounded cruel and distant, but I needed to be free from Abigail so I could finally move on. Without those divorce papers I would be tied to her forever. Abigail scrutinised me with a calculating look, before sighing like I was inconveniencing her and pulled a document file from her hidden safe. I watched diligently as she signed her name before handing them to me. I reached out to take them, but Abigail snatched them back.

"Who are you sleeping with?" she asked in a mocking tone.

"Whoever I like," I snarled, and snatched the papers that represented my escape route out of her hands.

"I know you Joe, you should be going into a mental tailspin right now, but instead, you can only think of moving on," she narrowed her eyes at me. "Have you been cheating on me, Joe?"

"Goodbye, Abigail," I pointedly ignored her questions, as after what she had done to me, she had no right to ask them. Then I did what I had wanted to do to Abigail for a long time; I turned my back on her and walked away.

"Wait!" Abigail's yell caught me as I had opened my car door. I was all set to ignore her until I heard the yapping of my two Highland Terriers. I was relieved to see Abigail had their leads on. "Don't you want to take them with you?" I watched suspicious as she led the dogs into the back seat of my car, and they were yipping excitedly at going on an adventure. This didn't sit right with me. Abigail never gave in unless something directly benefitted her, but I just couldn't tell what she wanted yet.

"Take care of them, ok?" she implored me earnestly before she enveloped me in a hug. I was so shocked by the warm gesture that I merely stood there frozen, until she released me. Abigail gave me a bashful nod before she ran back into the house to continue to try and escape the police. A prickle of unease went through me. Abigail had an ulterior motive here, but I just hadn't figured out what it was yet.

"Oh, and tell the chubby lawyer I'm sorry I threatened to reveal her secret," Abigail shrugged casually. And there it was, the reason she was out here. She had one last blow to deliver. "You know about how she killed that guy in Manchester."

"What?" I asked, stunned. Abigail smirked, and I knew I had fallen into her trap.

"You know that client she fucked who stalked her and attacked her? She ended up getting off with killing him in self-defence?" she gave a casual shrug, "give her my best," she called as she sashayed away from me. I was furious at how Abigail had managed to get one last psychological blow in and furious at

Laurel for not bothering to tell me any of this, as it gave Abigail the opportunity to hurt us both. It left me not knowing what the hell I was going to do next.

CHAPTER TWENTY

Joe

I walked into the tiny apartment I rented, my chest still thrumming with adrenaline. I couldn't tell you how I drove home, my body had been on complete autopilot while my brain had tried to take in everything that had happened. Abigail had stolen money. Abigail never loved me. I was divorced. Laurel had killed someone. I couldn't really absorb the information, it felt like it was happening to someone else, and I was watching from the sidelines, impassive. I needed a drink.

I crossed the apartment from the front door to the kitchen on the other side in ten paces. It was a tiny new build apartment that I was currently paying through the nose on rent for. It had been the first thing I could find when I left Abigail so I snapped it up. Embarrassingly the walls were all still cream-coloured and apart from a few necessary furnishings, like a sofa and a bed, it was pretty much bare and devoid of any sense that a functioning human being lived here, never mind a professional artist.

I opened the tiny fridge that looked ridiculously small in the designated space and pulled out a bottle of Budweiser and used the bottle opener on the side to pop it open. I took a satisfying gulp and the crisp bubbles flowed down my throat and melted away a little of my tension. I eyed my laptop on the sofa as Abigail's words rang through my brain. It couldn't hurt to just do a quick Google search and find out if she was lying, could it? My feet had taken me across the room, and my hands had opened the laptop and switched it on before I could really process the question.

My fingers hesitated over the keyboard—This was exactly what Abigail had wanted, to mess with my head and have me doubt Laurel. I couldn't just ask Laurel something like that because I would sound insane if it wasn't true. But what if it is true? A voice whispered in my head, and before I could think any further about it, my fingers flew over the keyboard, typing: 'Laurel Slater, murder, Manchester'. The search seemed to take eons to load but the headline results made my stomach turn.

'Solicitor kills defenceless man'
'Real life Basic Instinct'
'Killer solicitor fired from firm'

None of that sounded like the Laurel I knew, but maybe I never knew her at all. I needed to talk to her about this, I felt something for her, and I needed to hear the truth from her. But first, I needed to calm the fuck down. The only thing that could help calm my mind right now was drawing. It was how I channelled my emotions and worked through them. And I had way too many to work through right now. I discarded my beer in the kitchen, having only taken one mouthful and fished my car keys out of my pocket, and headed back out to my studio.

I pulled up into the industrial unit's car park, and something just felt... off. Everything looked normal but my senses were all on high alert. There are lots of small businesses on this lot, from a PT studio to a rehearsal space for a band, so a few cars parked around was normal. As I got out of my car, I walked slowly and carefully towards the front door of my studio, waiting for someone to spring out of the darkness at me, but it didn't happen. My heart sunk as I saw the front door move slightly in the gentle breeze. I took in the smashed lock and gently pulled the door open, nervous about what I would find inside.

My studio was trashed. My brushes were scattered across the floor, and scraps of drawings from my sketchbooks were littered everywhere. My stools, desk and easels had all been knocked over, making it look like a bomb had gone off. Anything I was working on had been ruined and was in tatters on the ground. My painting of Laurel was barely recognisable, as a few scraps had been littered around an easel. Devastation washed over me, followed by overwhelming rage. Someone came into my private space and destroyed one of the few things I cared about. My foot kicked out and sent a stool sailing across the room with a satisfying crash. I was going to kill whoever did this.

I searched my pockets to find my phone to call the police but came up empty. I pat each of my pockets one more time to check if I missed it but I hadn't. I hadn't seen it since before I went into Seven Deadly Sins a few hours ago. Who the fuck had stolen my phone?

CHAPTER TWENTY-ONE

Laurel

The next day I practically sprang out of bed, anxious and excited for the day ahead. Abigail should have been arrested at some point last night, and Joe was surely going to see Abigail today and make her sign the divorce papers nicely and quietly. I'm sure of it. I know he had stormed out of Seven Deadly Sins when he heard the news about Abigail; he probably wanted to be alone, and I could understand that. Once that was all closed off, Joe could finally get his two dogs back, and I could finally ask him on a date, a real date, and not feel guilty about it. Today things could finally start going right for me. I hummed happily as I showered, threw on a pretty, open-backed sun dress and sandals, and left my hair loose. I checked my phone for any messages from Joe, but nothing yet, he was probably still busy, and I didn't want to seem like a nutcase by texting him all the time. I buried my head in working on a marketing plan to get some clients and make a more reliable income for my practice. Two hours later, and I still hadn't heard from Joe, tendrils of doubt began to curl around my thoughts. Busy, I needed to keep busy. I traipsed downstairs and started cleaning the reception area, making sure to get every last speck of dust. I even cleaned the skirting boards and hoovered the sofa crevices.

Two more hours had passed, and still nothing from Joe. Had I read everything wrong between us? Now he had his divorce, was he done with me? I had naively thought he might feel something for me or at least that he would call me to let me know how things went. Feeling desperate and needy and not in my usual good way, I caved into temptation and texted Joe.

Hi! How did it go? I hoped it came across as light and breezy. My phone pinged a reply less than a minute later and I sighed with relief—until I read the message.

We're done, Lauren. Lauren? Was it an auto-correct of my name? Or did he genuinely not care about me at all? I decided to give him the benefit of the doubt.

How are the dogs? I asked, just to keep the conversation going and to hopefully get a friendlier reply.

Well, they look better than you at least, but that's not hard. Hurt and shame washed over me. Joe knew how self-conscious I was about my body, and I had no idea what I had done to deserve these cruel words.

Did I do something wrong? I couldn't help but ask, even though I knew it made me sound desperate. I thought we had understood each other. I thought we had both felt something between us. I felt my throat constrict in fear—this couldn't be happening! Joe wasn't like this.

No, I got what I needed. I don't have to pretend to be into you anymore. Tears pricked at the corners of my eyes as I pressed the call button, needing to hear it from him rather than as text on a screen. I wanted to hear the tone in his voice when he said those things to me. It just didn't seem like him, but maybe I never knew him at all. The call rang twice before it abruptly cut off. I dialled again, and it went straight to voicemail. And again. And again. I knew I was coming off as slightly insane and desperate, but I didn't care. I needed to know what I did wrong. A text finally pings through.

I'm not taking your calls. Take the hint. I know what you did, you psycho. I'm blocking your number. The tears started to fall freely down my cheeks, and my vision blurred as I slumped to the floor. I felt ridiculous—I got myself all dressed up and expected some kind of romance novel ending. I've been so naive and stupid that I expected a sexual BDSM relationship with a client just getting divorced to turn into a real relationship. After the terrible things I had done, I didn't deserve a happy ending. How could anyone feel anything for a monster like me?

CHAPTER TWENTY-TWO

Laurel

Two days later, I looked at myself in the mirror and took my appearance in for the first time. My eyes were red and puffy, and the rest of my skin was nearly grey with exhaustion. I hadn't slept since Joe had written those true but horrible things, and I hadn't done much of anything apart from moping and staring into space. I had the TV on sometimes just to break the silence that surrounded me until it turned itself off again. I had no idea what was even on. I know I'm pathetic and that just made me feel even more despair. My hair was greasy and sticking out everywhere. It's not just about Joe ditching me, but every self-doubt I had ever felt about myself he threw back at me and validated, and by someone I had trusted. I had felt like a monster before—Joe had just confirmed it, and the last shred of hope that I had clung to that I could one day have a normal relationship had been torn to pieces.

My phone rang several times over those two days, but I didn't even want to look at it. No one should have to put up with a monster like me. I became vaguely aware of someone knocking on my door repeatedly, and I tried to ignore them by holding throw cushions on each of my ears, but they didn't stop. I turned the TV up so loud it made me wince, but still, they kept on knocking. I sighed in resignation and hauled myself onto my feet.

It took all my effort to drag myself to the door and to put a false smile on my face as I opened it. Bella's worried face reached me through the evening gloom.

"Are you sick?" she asked, taking in my unkept appearance, "you weren't answering your phone, so I was worried." I felt incredibly guilty. Here I was making people miserable again. I was like a disease that wouldn't stop spreading.

"I'm a monster, so Joe ended things," I croaked pathetically.

"Oh, sweetheart," she sighed and enveloped me in a warm hug. Feeling her try to comfort me in my despondent state prompted me to burst into floods of tears all over again, my body going limp as we dropped to the floor. "It will be ok," she tried to soothe me, as she ignored the discomfort of my doorstep beneath our knees. I didn't have the heart to tell her how wrong she was.

When I had finally calmed down enough for Bella to half carry me upstairs with her arm wrapped around my shoulders to hold me upright—I let her. She dropped me heavily onto the sofa, where I curled back up in a protective ball and wrapped a blanket tightly around myself. I refusing to make eye contact with her. She pottered around my kitchen and after a few minutes, appeared with two steaming cups of tea.

"Tell me what that arsehole did," Bella ordered in a tone that sent a shiver down my spine.

"It's not what he did. It's what I did," I mumbled and clutched the blanket tighter around myself like it could protect me from the world. I risked a glance at Bella's face and saw nothing but concern there, and I savoured that moment because I was probably never going to see it directed at me again. "I didn't tell you the whole truth when I told you about Manchester." I left that small admission hanging in the air between us.

"I felt like something didn't add up with the story. Are you ready to share the rest with me now?" Bella asks me calmly. She had settled herself onto the sofa with her legs crossed and casually sipped her tea.

"You might as well as know, as I'm sure the truth is going to be everywhere soon," I sighed, feeling utterly defeated and hopeless. "There really was a guy who went to the bosses of my old firm and got me sacked for sleeping with him, but he didn't stop there." Bella's hand reached across and squeezed mine encouragingly. I drew in a breath to gather my confidence and kept going. "He would start showing up everywhere I went, the gym, the supermarket, even job interviews he would be somewhere outside. He never said anything to me, just stood nearby and smiled at me when I looked at him—it was the creepiest thing ever," I couldn't help but shudder at the memory.

"Didn't you go to the police?" Bella asked gently.

"Yes, but I was so upset they thought I was crazy, and when they questioned him, he made them believe I was the one following him!" I didn't think I had any tears left but I'm surprised to feel more pouring down my face.

"How could they even think that?" Bella shouted in disgust, making me wince.

"Who would you believe—the seemingly sane guy with a good job and a normal life or a psycho-looking woman with no job who was fired for having sex with a client and was drowning in debt? I know I wouldn't have believed me either back then. So I stopped leaving my house altogether. I put high walls around my house so no one could see in, the neighbours complained, but I felt safer. I got one of those work-from-home customer service jobs, and anything I needed I had delivered, but that must have just pissed him off, because about a month later, he decided to break in."

"Holy shit! I hope they believed you then!"

"They didn't get the chance to," I sighed, "he told me I had made us a perfect hideaway where we could be alone and no one would ever disturb us. He kept me tied up for three days until I finally saw an opportunity and used a pocket knife to cut through the rope. I don't know what came over me but I was just so desperate and so angry. I picked up a huge knife from my kitchen and surprised him, stabbing him until he stopped moving."

"I'm so sorry you went through that, Laurel," Bella told me as she squeezed my hand again, and I looked up at her in shock.

"You don't think I'm a monster?"

"Fuck no!" She exclaimed, "I think the guy that did that to you is a monster. I think you're the bravest person I know for being able to start your life over after that, and you're kind of a badass too."

"Yeah, I'm a real badass," I pointed to myself in my dirty sweatpants and oversized t-shirt.

"Well, not right now, but in general, yeah," she shrugged with a small smile.

"You really don't think I'm a terrible person?"

"Definitely not, but I'm wondering what this has to do with you and Joe?"

"Joe made me feel sexy and wanted, but it was never a 'normal' relationship, you know? And that's all I've ever really wanted. I wanted to talk to him about how I felt and if we could try dating outside of SDS, but his wife must have told him what I did in Manchester, so he ended things with me by text."

"What a dick."

"I have no idea what the hell to do now. It feels like everything is falling down around me all over again," I said in a hollow voice.

"Well, first thing, we need to get you a shower and a toothbrush because, no offence, sweetie, but you stink," I couldn't help the giggle that escaped at her words. "Then we get you to bed to rest, and tomorrow morning we look at your business and how we can make it grow. Your happiness is not defined by any man, got it?" She barked and waggled her finger at me to emphasise her point.

"Yes, ma'am," I submitted, making us both giggle again. God, it felt good to have everything off my chest and have someone finally believe me. Maybe I could make my life here work.

CHAPTER TWENTY-THREE

Laurel

Three days later a hammering on my door brought me out of my stupor. I stumbled towards the door, my eyes blurry from staring at my laptop screen.

"Joe!?" I exclaim in surprise, seeing his scowling face when I open the door. "Don't worry I got the message, you don't need to hammer it home," I sighed, moving to close the door. Joe shoved the door open again, looking furious.

"What the fuck are you talking about?" he growled, walking into my flat and slamming the door shut.

"Look, I get it—you got my help getting rid of Abigail, and now you don't want to see me anymore, granted a text message was a shitty way to do it..." I shrugged, but he cut me off.

"Text message? I lost my phone a few days ago. What the fuck are you talking about?" he gripped my forearms and stared into my eyes, looking utterly confused but still raging.

"You sent me all those mean texts," I mumbled, feeling slightly juvenile.

"When?" he snarled.

"The day after you left Seven Deadly Sins," I answered tentatively, jumping when Joe let out a snarl of anger.

"I went to see Abigail, so she must have stolen my phone," he explained through gritted teeth, "I've been waiting at Seven Deadly Sins every night and coming to the shop every day trying to run into you. I thought you didn't want to see me until your friend just stormed up to me in SDS last night and bollocked me for dumping you."

"So, you didn't say those things?" I was still trying to wrap my head around things.

"No," Joe told me firmly as he brought one of his hands up to cup my cheek, "and I definitely didn't want to end things with you."

"Oh," I sighed. Emotions swirled inside me as I tried to make sense of what was happening, relief, excitement, panic, and anger at Abigail. Before I could delve into any of those feelings, Joe's lips met mine, and nothing else mattered. His kisses were hard and demanding, and my body instinctually submitted to him, my knees weak as I gripped his arms to hold myself up.

"Bedroom, now," Joe ordered when we finally broke apart. My feet moved on submissive instinct and took me into my bedroom to wait for more orders. "Lie down, hands on the headboard until I say so." Taking orders from him again had every part of my body singing in satisfaction as I lay down. My sweatpants and underwear were roughly tugged off, and he buried his face in my bare crotch. Joe slowly licked a line up my slit before he sucked on my clit. I was in heaven. His thumb began gently probing at my anus, and I let out a strangled moan as he breached the tight hole. He started a gentle rhythm with his thumb as he continued sucking on my clit, leaving me gasping and writhing. My orgasm built quickly, and I threw my head back to welcome it when Joe abruptly stopped moving.

"Whatever happened in the past for either of us doesn't matter," he whispered, his breath warm on my overstimulated clit, and I couldn't help but wiggle in frustration. "We begin now, no more secrets, no more lies, agreed?"

"Yes!" I screamed out, frantic for him to continue his delicious torture of my body. A whimper escaped me as Joe removed his thumb, but he quickly inserted two fingers in its place, scissoring and stretching me. I had no idea where he got lube from and when he applied it, but my brain couldn't keep up with everything happening around me.

"What happened in Manchester?" he growled, and I flinched, hesitating. "No secrets," he repeated as if sensing I was thinking of telling a half-truth.

"I dated one of my clients," I finally wailed, "but he went crazy and started stalking me." Normally confessing anything like this brought up a whirlwind of negative emotions—but my mind was already overwhelmed by Joe's probing fingers and wicked tongue, as he lapped at my clit as a reward for telling the truth. I needed to keep going if I wanted more. "He got me fired and didn't have an excuse to see me anymore, so he started going everywhere I went. When I stopped leaving my house, he broke in." I couldn't help but lose my train of thought as Joe nibbled that sensitive bundle of nerves that had me arching off the bed. "I didn't say stop," came his barked order. I picked out a dark spot on my ceiling to focus on and kept myself on track as I started talking again.

"The night he broke in, he was insane. He tied me up and kept me prisoner for days, I had a chance to escape, but I killed him first so he couldn't hurt me anymore." I was telling my deepest, darkest secret out loud for only the second time and I didn't care, I was nearing the edge of the abyss of pleasure, and nothing outside of me and Joe seemed to exist. I writhed in pleasure, my hands gripping the headboard for dear life rather than disobey him and let go.

"Tell me what you want," he growled.

"I want to be yours!" I cried out. I think he expected me to ask for an orgasm, but I instinctively asked for what I wanted, to belong to him. Joe removed his fingers and lifted my legs, lining up his huge hard cock with my needy pussy. I had no idea when he shed his pants and underwear, but I lost all mental competency as his cock slid inside for a few quick thrusts before he slid out and started to push into my arse. My juices eased the way a little, but it was still a squeeze and slow going as Joe kept gently thrust to stretch me until I finally felt his balls rest on my arse cheeks.

He was knelt on the bed, my legs wrapped around him like a pretzel, and his cock buried into my arse as he gazed down at me in adoration. With this angle, I couldn't take all of him, but right now, this is about him reasserting his Dominance over me. "You are mine." It came out as an animalistic snarl, showing how close he was to the edge of his own restraint. I nodded my consent. I've always been his—he ruined me for any other man the first time our eyes locked. His grip tightened on my hips, and he began hammering into me. My nerve endings were crackling. No build-up to this brutal pace, I was his to fuck, and he wanted to fuck my arse hard to remind me who I belonged to, and I loved every second. It felt so much more intimate like this with him on top of me rather than behind me, our eyes glued to each other as he plundered such a taboo place. Sweat dripped from his brow, mussing up his hair as soft grunts of pleasure left his lips. Joe reached up and freed one of my hands from where it still gripped the headboard for dear life.

"Pinch your clit and come with me," he growled, losing the battle for his control, and I loved that I could do that to him. With an animalistic growl, Joe came deep inside me—his eyes narrowing as he stayed focused on watching me pinch my clit. It was the most erotic experience I have ever had, and the burning pleasure overwhelmed me as I had the best orgasm of my life. I was still panting and coming down from my high as Joe pulled out of me and climbed off the bed heading towards the bedroom door.

"Come on, good girl, you can join me in the shower and clean us both off," I felt myself becoming aroused again at the thought of seeing him dripping wet and getting to clean him. We had showered together before, but I had been half asleep and hadn't truly appreciate it. I was his, I belonged to him, and I was catapulted to a new level of arousal at that thought. "Then I'm going to fuck some sense into you over lying to me about Manchester." I shivered in excitement. I couldn't fucking wait.

CHAPTER TWENTY-FOUR

Joe

Laurel is coiled around me, her head resting on my chest, and the sense of warmth and comfort I felt was unfamiliar to me. I meant what I said to her. I didn't care what had happened to her before we met—I only wanted to focus on who we were now.

"You look deep in thought," Laurel mumbled against my chest. I turned my head slightly to take in the soft smile on her face, and her beautiful brown eyes gazed at me affectionately.

"I was just thinking I meant what I said earlier, that our pasts are behind us, and it's a fresh start for us," I told her as I dropped an affectionate kiss on her forehead. A month ago, this was a place I swore I would never end up again, falling for a woman and giving them the power to hurt me so brutally again, but Laurel made me not care about any of that. I would go through all that pain again just to spend time with her like this.

"Yeah," she mumbled quietly, her eyes going down to my chest, where her fingers weaved an intricate pattern.

"Hey," I grasped her chin and forced her to look up at me, "I mean it." I lowered my mouth to hers, kissing her furiously to reassure her physically as well as verbally, and she readily returned my kiss and hummed in satisfaction.

"Okay," she agreed when I finally released her. Damn, her kisses were addictive and made my dick start stirring again already.

"So, I was thinking we should go out tomorrow night," I said as casually as I could.

"Out?" Laurel echoed sounding puzzled. I cringed internally at how bad I was at this. Giving orders during sex I was a master at, but asking a woman on a date, and I suddenly felt like I was twelve years old again asking a girl out who was way out of my league and fearing rejection.

"A date," I blurted out before I wince at my cowardice. I felt Laurel shift her position so she was sat up and could look at me, and I hesitantly opened my eyes and found her brown ones searching my face. I don't know what they were looking for, but she seemed torn by what she finds.

"Like as in a romantic date as a couple or as a Master and submissive date?" She asked with an edge to her tone. Holy fuck, I was making a huge mess of this. I growled in frustration and scrubbed my hands down my face to shake off my fears, and Laurel startled in surprise.

"As in a romantic date, as in get to know me as someone you would consider being a boyfriend date, as in be mine exclusively to date," I blurted out before I could overthink it too much. God, it felt good to call her mine, with the knowledge that if she agreed, she would be mine and only mine.

"Oh," she said as her eyebrows reached her hairline. Oh fuck, she doesn't want that, and now I've made a complete mess of this whole thing. "Then yes, I'm in." It took a few seconds for my brain to process her reply.

"Thank God!" I cheered as I pulled her to me for another heated kiss.

Painting Gluttony

I won't lie, I agonised all day yesterday about where to take Laurel tonight. Nothing felt like it was good enough for her. I wanted to talk to her, to get to know her outside of the drama and the mind-blowing sex. So I went with a tapas restaurant and frantically made the reservation half an hour ago when I was spun out and desperate. A tapas restaurant seems cheesy and dull, but I could actually talk to Laurel there, and it wouldn't come off like I was trying too hard.

I pulled into the tiny car park behind Laurel's flat, and she came flouncing out of the front door straight away, making me scramble to get out and hold the passenger door open for her. Holy shit. She was wearing the tiny black dress from the night we met. The dress that has been in some of my fantasies where I rewatch her lift it over her head to reveal herself to me.

"I thought you might like this dress," she smirked at me whilst sliding into the car. The temptress knew exactly what she was doing and knew she had me hard as a fucking rock already. My hand itched to spank her as both a reward and punishment for teasing me.

"Minx," I replied, and she just laughed as I closed the door. It was the first time I had really seen Laurel like this, so relaxed and joking with me, and I couldn't help but realise I was falling a little harder for her.

CHAPTER TWENTY-FIVE

Laurel

Pulling up to the Tapas restaurant, I had to say I was a little relieved. This dress was not meant to be worn for things like bowling, and I did kind of worry that with Joe being an artist, he would have come up with something quirky for our first date. But Tapas was easy and made me instantly feel a little more relaxed.

The look on Joe's face when I had walked out my door wearing this dress again still made a stupid grin break out on my face when I thought of it. He looked at me like I was beautiful, and as long as that was true for him, I didn't really care what anyone else thought. Joe looked devastatingly handsome in black trousers and a black short-sleeved shirt that had the top few buttons undone. I just wanted to lean down and lick the exposed skin. I had never seen him out of a pair of his trademark jeans, and I couldn't decide which look did it for me more. And his cologne. Holy hell. Getting into the car had me wrapped in the woodsy, masculine scent that made my lower body clench like he was wearing pheromones.

Joe parked the car and shot around it to open my door for me. Say what you want, but being a gentleman like that never went out of fashion, and it made a goofy grin appear on my face at being treated so respectfully. My hand slid into his as he helped me out of the car and kept my hand securely in his as he led me inside. I could barely contain my glee that this was happening. I thought I would never be able to date a normal guy again, not with him knowing about who I was and what I've done, yet here I am, hand in hand with an amazing guy.

As soon as we walked inside, the smell of all the gorgeous food made my stomach rumble, and I hoped no one else heard it over the salsa music playing in the background. I have never been here before, but the restaurant looked cosy, decorated in red and gold, with little tables dotted around in cosy alcoves.

"Table for Hamilton," Joe asked the server as he approached us, waving us to follow him to a cute little booth for two. I sank down onto the luxurious fabric of the bench as Joe settled opposite me.

"Can I start you off with some drinks?" The waiter asked us.

"Lemonade," we both replied in sync before sharing a nervous laugh. The waiter grinned and retreated, leaving us in a slightly awkward silence.

"How was your day?" Joe asked me to break the tension.

"Good," I replied lamely, wracking my brain for anything to say about it but drawing a blank. "How was yours?"

"Good," he replied, looking around the restaurant for some sort of conversational inspiration.

"What have you been working on?" I asked tentatively.

"Well, my studio was absolutely trashed the night Abigail was going to be arrested."

"Wait! What? Why didn't you tell me?" I exclaimed, feeling hurt.

"I was too busy fucking your brains out," he told me with a smug smile that made me blush to the roots of my hair. The waiter chose that moment to deliver our drinks, and Joe ordered us a few dishes to start with as I was clearly unable to form a sentence at that point. Once the waiter had left and my brain was back in control of my body, I finally got out "So your studio was trashed?"

"Yes," he sighed, looking lost, so I reached over the table to squeeze his hand in reassurance. "I think it might have been Abigail. Nothing was taken, just trashed."

"I thought she was going to be arrested?"

"Oh well, she managed to slip away from the police. They are still trying to find her," he shrugged, and I felt my own anger at Abigail bubble to the surface. I knew she was a bitch, but to do something so petty and hurtful was beyond what I thought she was capable of. "Anyway, with us having a fresh start together, I wanted to give you a present." He reached into his pocket and pulled out a small envelope and slid it over the table to me. I rushed to tear it open, and something that looked like a credit card dropped out. A membership card to Seven Deadly Sins. He had got me my own membership card.

I glanced down at the shiny black card and tried to school my features into a pleased reaction. Joe obviously thought this was a nice gift to give me and I didn't want to hurt his feelings, but this was possibly the most confusing thing he could have done. I thought we were going to give a real relationship a try, but this just reminded me that he liked to be a Dominant and wanted a submissive. Although I've enjoyed the kinky sex we've had, that isn't all I want in a relationship. Joe could take a guest in with his card, and by giving me my own, it meant he expected me to go to SDS without him. It also meant he intended to go without me. Another thing I hadn't expected. I'd thought Joe asking me to go on a 'real date' meant he wanted to be with me and just me, but clearly, I was wrong again. Tears pricked at the corners of my eyes, and a lump swelled in my throat, but I pushed it all down and forced myself to smile at Joe.

"Thank you, it's great." I managed to push the words out.

CHAPTER TWENTY-SIX

Joe

"Thank you, it's great." Her reaction wasn't what I expected at all. Laurel was trying to convince us both that she liked the gift, but I could see the hurt in her eyes, and my chest clenched in dismay. I could almost swear she was holding back tears, but I couldn't be certain. I knew she was new, but surely she understood what a big thing it was that I was giving her my SDS membership card? Then I could only ever go there with her if she wanted to go. If she didn't ever want to go again, that's fine with me as long as we were together. Her second gift burned a hole in my pocket, but her reaction to the card had thrown me. I thought she was just as invested in us as I was, but maybe I was moving too fast. Maybe I was repeating the mistakes I made with Abigail? I mentally shook myself, as Laurel was nothing like Abigail.

The waiter appeared with our food, and another awkward silence descended between us. I had done something wrong, but I had no clue what or how to fix it. The food smelt delicious, and I started to pick at it while I tried to engage Laurel in conversation, trying any topic I could think of, but she just gave me short answers and pushed her food around her plate, barely eating anything. I hardly ate anything either—I was so torn up over Laurel's actions that even my favourite dishes didn't appeal to me.

"Was your food okay?" The waiter asked nervously as he came to collect our nearly full plates.

"Yeah, everything was great. We're just not hungry. Can we get the bill please?" The waiter looked between myself and Laurel, picked up on the tension and scarpered away. He was back with our bill in less than a minute. I gave the guy a huge tip for sparing me more awareness at this table, as I dropped the cash on the table and stood. Laurel silently stood, grabbed her purse and followed me out the door. This was officially the most awkward date I had ever been on. I needed to get us back on track.

"Do you want to come back to my place?" I asked nervously. Maybe if we were alone somewhere I could find out what the hell was going on.

"Your place?" She asked, seeming surprised, but a tiny smile graced her features for the first time in an hour, so I was obviously doing something right again.

"Yeah, I feel like I am always staying with you, and you've never seen my place," I shrugged as I tried to sound as casual as my nerves would let me.

"Sure, let's go." There was that tiny smile again. Maybe I was worrying over nothing.

Laurel

Okay, I was a bit thrown off by him inviting me to his place at first. It felt like we were taking a big step forwards and that I was worrying over nothing. Until I saw it. The blandness and emptiness of it told me he didn't really live here or care about this place. It was obviously just somewhere he brought casual hookups. His dogs weren't even here.

"Can I get you a drink or anything?" He asked, sounding slightly uncomfortable.

"No, I'm good." I threw my jacket off and onto the sofa and did a lap of the living room to confirm my suspicions that this isn't really Joe's home. I settled on the sofa, and Joe dropped next to me—the silence became deafening.

"Did I say or do something wrong, Laurel?" Joe finally asked.

"No, I'm just a little tired," my lie sounded weak, but I didn't want to fight with him.

"I can take you home if you'd like?"

"It would seem a shame for your bachelor pad not to see any action. That's its main purpose, right?" I couldn't help but snap, my anger leaked out despite his offer sounding genuine.

"What's that supposed to mean?" He sounded annoyed now too. I suppose I was being a complete bitch, but I couldn't seem to stop myself.

"This is where you bring women to sleep with them, right? Wouldn't want to disappoint."

"No one has ever been in here before..."

"Oh, so this a special fuck pad just for me? I'm honoured," I sniped sarcastically and Joe's face turned furious.

"Look, I hope you're not implying that this between us is meaningless to me?"

"What am I supposed to think? You imply you want to see other people by giving me that stupid card, then bring me to somewhere that you obviously don't live..."

"I do live here!" He yelled and I felt tears prick at the corners of my eyes. I wouldn't let him see me cry. I forced the tears back with all the willpower I had.

"Then where are your photos? Or personal items? There's a surprising lack of art for a so-called artist. Or what about your dogs, the ones you made me fight so hard to get you?" He let out a frustrated sigh and raked his fingers through his hair, not answering any of my questions and in doing so, he answered all of them.

"I'm out of here," I declared, angrily putting my coat on.

Painting Gluttony

"Laurel! Wait! I really don't..." he shouted, chasing me down the corridor. I cut him off as I slammed his front door in his face, feeling a smidge of satisfaction as the tears finally started to fall.

CHAPTER TWENTY-SEVEN

Joe

I found my SDS membership posted through my letterbox before I left for my studio the next morning, with Ant and Dec in tow. I chose to walk there today as I needed to think, and the dynamic duo needed some exercise. They tugged on their lead slightly in their eagerness to find out what had changed in the world since their last walk, and my other hand slipped into my pocket to graze against the black card that seemed to weigh me down.

I had no idea what happened last night. I had tried to plan things as well as I could. I had even asked my neighbour to take care of the dogs in case we spent the night at Laurel's. Everything seemed fine at first, and then something in Laurel just changed. Last night I was furious about the things she accused me of. But five minutes after she slammed the door in my, face I realised she had left alone and with no car. No matter how angry I was, I didn't want her to get hurt. After I sprinted up and down my street in search of her, I had called and texted her constantly until she finally answered and said she was home safely before slamming the phone down on me again.

Now that I had a clearer head, I had no idea where I stood with Laurel, but I knew that I wasn't going to give her up. My feet had been on autopilot while my mind raced, and they hadn't taken me to my studio. Laurel's name across the window glittered in the sunlight. Fuck my life. My subconscious was giving me a not-so-subtle hint. I peered through the window, looking and feeling like a complete stalker.

Laurel was talking to a tall blonde woman I didn't recognise in the waiting room. She looked calm and relaxed as she spoke, but I could see the slight redness around her eyes from either lack of sleep, crying or both, and I winced guiltily. Both women turned in sync to see me staring through the window at them, the other woman looked startled, but Laurel narrowed her eyes at me in annoyance. Unsure what else to do in this scenario, I gave them both a tentative wave, and Laurel rolled her eyes at me. The woman moved to leave, and I drew in a steadying breath, nodding a greeting to her as she looked on in amusement as Ant, Dec and I crossed the threshold into the shop.

"I came to apologise!" I blurted as I held up my hands in surrender.

"Okay," she said slowly, "what are you apologising for?" The question was a dangerous one. The way she eyed me suspiciously had me frozen in fear.

"I don't really know," I confessed, deciding honesty is the best policy rather than trying to guess. "But I know I hurt you, and that's something I never wanted to do." Dec was sniffing Laurel's feet, and she seemed to be fighting a smile at his friendliness. "If you tell me what I did, I promise to try and make it right." She bent down to cuddle Dec, not caring about her nice clothes getting dirty paw prints on them, which made me even more attracted to her. She chewed her lip for a moment like she was debating what to say, so I waited patiently until she stood and looked into my eyes again.

Painting Gluttony

"I thought you had asked me on a real date, and being taken to that flat that wasn't yours made me feel really cheap," she confessed, and it was like a punch to the gut.

"That is my flat. I just knew it was temporary, so I never bothered buying furniture or decorating or anything," I shrugged and rubbed the back of my neck to try and alleviate some of the tension there.

"Why weren't your dogs there then?" She asked, looking pointedly down at them and then back at me.

"I asked my neighbour to look after them, in case you wanted to go to your place."

"Oh," she looked stunned.

"But there was something going on before that. You were acting all weird in the restaurant. What happened?" Laurel buried her face in her hands, turning slightly red.

"Okay, so you gave me my membership card to Seven Deadly Sins, and it made me realise that you wanted me to go there without you, meaning you wanted to go without me, and that's not what I thought I was getting into and it hurt my feelings a little." Fuck. I should have given her the second gift.

"You miss understood me, Laurel," I sighed in defeat, "it wasn't a membership card for you. It was mine."

Laurel

"What?" I asked, struggling to wrap my head around what was happening. "Why would I want yours?"

"It was my way of trying to tell you that I only ever want to be there with you," my heart hammered in my chest at his words. "It was also me giving up control to you of if you ever want to go there again."

"But you like to be in charge..."

"I know, but I was gifting that to you," he smiled gently at me.

"Oh," I mumbled, stunned into silence for a few seconds before I exclaimed: "OH!" The full weight of his gift finally sank in.

"So, what do you think? Can we have a do-over date tonight?" He asked with a soft smile that I just couldn't say no to.

"Why do you still want me?" Flew out of my mouth before I could help it. He dropped the leads on the floor and his dogs took off to explore my office behind us as Joe cupped my cheek in one of his huge hands.

Painting Gluttony

"Because you're the most beautiful woman I have ever met, both inside and out, and I can't stop thinking about you," his thumb swiped across my bottom lip as my heart stuttered at his words. "So, can we try again tonight?"

"Yes," I agreed instantly, nodding my head emphatically too. I had gotten everything all wrong the other night, and I definitely wanted to see where this could go.

CHAPTER TWENTY-EIGHT

Joe

I fixed my gaze on Laurel as she removed her coat. She was wearing that damn black dress again, taunting me with all her curves that I couldn't touch in this place. She knew that dress made me lose my mind, so she was trying to goad me. I shot her a look.

"What? You picked the same restaurant, I can't pick the same dress?" She smiled and shrugged at me before she slid into the booth. I did pick the same restaurant because I thought I could make a joke about it being a do-over, but the little minx beat me to it. Damn, that's hot.

Painting Gluttony

The same waiter walked over to us with menus, and I cursed my bad luck. I was hoping for a different server that had no idea we had an argument and had left without eating last night.

"Two lemonades, please," I requested with a tight smile. Both Laurel and the waiter looked at me in amusement, but neither said anything so the waiter left to get the drinks.

"Ordering for me now?" Laurel quipped as soon as he was out of earshot.

"I just wanted him to leave us alone," I shrugged, sliding into the seat on the opposite side of the booth.

"Two lemonades," the waiter announced as he placed the drinks in front of us before hastily retreating again. If he kept this up, I would probably need to leave him a huge tip this time.

"Before he comes back, I wanted to give you something."

"Do all your presents need explanations so they don't upset me?" Laurel shot me a cheeky smile. That's actually kind of true, so I fished the black velvet box about the size of my fist out of my jacket and slid it across the table to her. She looked startled at the appearance of the box and hesitantly pulled it over to her like it might suddenly explode.

I watched her open the jewellery box and saw a soft smile on her face. A wave of relief rushed through my body.

"It's beautiful," she sighed, "but it's not just a necklace, is it?" She asked as her big brown eyes looked at me questioningly.

"No," I admitted, "I'm not sure if you've heard of collaring before?" A blush flooded her cheeks instantly, and I knew she had. "Well, think of this as an alternative to a collar. You wear it everywhere and let everyone see that you are mine. You will always let me be in charge. Do you want that, Laurel?"

"Yes," her voice was barely above a whisper. Her eyes were almost black and blown with arousal as she lifted the delicate chain out of the box. "Will you?" She offered the chain to me, and I sighed in satisfaction.

"It would be my honour," I arose from my chair and circled behind her like a predator stalking his prey. I brushed her locks to the side, inhaling the faint smell of her coconut shampoo, and draped the chain around her neck, fastening it securely. I circled back to my chair and took in the breathtaking sight of Laurel wearing my initials around her throat. Mine. The world narrowed down to just the two of us.

"Get back in the car," I snarled.

Painting Gluttony

"But we haven't eaten yet," Laurel stuttered.

"Back in the car now, or I fuck you over this table and let everyone watch." I was in full Dom mode, and I needed Laurel. Now. I threw some money on the table and yanked her arm to have her hurry after me. Fresh air blasted into my lungs as we finally reached the parking lot.

"Wow, me wearing your initials really does it for you, huh?" She asked with that sultry smile on her face. I wrapped my fingers in her hair and pulled her to me in a bruising kiss. "Mine," I snarled.

"Not yet," she smirked, and I felt my heart sink a little, "You'll have to catch me first." She shoved me hard enough to make me stumble backwards, and then she took off running into the woods. I have never thought about primal play much, but the sight of Laurel racing away from me into the dense woodland had my inner predator rising to the surface and me hard as a rock.

"Fuck," I cursed how hot this was before stalking after Laurel into the dark.

CHAPTER TWENTY-NINE

Laurel

My heart hammered as I raced through the trees, quickly losing the unnatural lighting of the car park and having to rely on the light of the moon to keep me from tripping. I didn't know what made me start this game, but adrenaline mixed with arousal made me feel more alive than I had ever felt. I caught sight of a really old-looking tree with a huge trunk and used it as a hiding spot to catch my breath.

I heard the cracking of twigs as Joe chased after me.

"Come out now and your punishment will be light," Joe called as he slowed to a walk, searching for me amongst the trees. The thought of a punishment made my lower body clench. But I didn't want him to go easy on me, and I wasn't going to go easy on him—I enjoyed this game far too much. With a small shriek of excitement, I took off again through the trees, and Joe's soft chuckle rang in my ears as I sprinted off—the speed made my hair whip out behind me and caused me to feel freer than I ever had before.

The wind was knocked out of me as Joe tackled me to the floor after he had snuck up beside me. Joe turned us, so he took the impact of hitting the ground and then rolled us so I was pinned underneath him.

"Now you're going to be punished, Laurel," he crooned in my ear—his warm breath sent shivers of anticipation down my spine. He sat back on his knees and I saw an opportunity to try to crawl away and escape. As soon as I turned my body, Joe hauled me back and pressed my back against his chest, both of us on our knees as his cock dug into my arse.

"Do you know how predictable you are, little prey?" He whispered in my ear as his lips gently brushed against the sensitive skin. I shivered as he called me prey—the idea was both terrifying and arousing. His strong hands forced me to bend over so I was on my hands and knees for him, before he skimmed delicate little trails up the inside of my thigh, finally landing on my soaked knickers. I felt a sharp tug, and the sound of material tearing told me my poor underwear has been shredded. The cold air nipped at my entire bottom half as my dress as hiked up around my waist.

There was no foreplay or prewarning for me as I felt Joe line his cock up with my entrance. No, right now, he was a predator that had caught his prey, and he was going to do whatever he wanted with me. In one hard thrust, he sheathed himself inside me, and I cried out at the heady mix of pain and pleasure. I was soaked but without any foreplay to ease the way Joe's cock felt huge, and I swear I could feel every vein and ridge as he rubbed along my overly sensitised walls. One of his hands wrapped in my hair, making me hold my head tilted back whilst his other hand was firmly on my hip, holding me in place. Joe fucked me at a brutal pace, but every time I neared the edge of an orgasm, he abruptly stopped until it receded, before pounding into me again. I was a sweating, writhing mess on my knees in the dirt while this powerful alpha predator thrust into me from behind. I was babbling and begging him to let me come, but he just chuckled and increased his torture on my body.

"Mine," he snarled as his grip tightened on my hair. He must have been nearing his own release, and I was desperate to join him.

"Yes! Yours!" I told him, and it was clearly the right thing to say. "Mine," he cried again, pounding into me relentlessly before he shuddered to his release. I could only scream my agreement as I catapulted over the edge of my own orgasm, and my limbs trembled uncontrollably. We both collapsed in a heap on the ground, gasping for breath but unwilling to let go of each other.

"That was... unexpected," Joe laughed when he finally caught his breath.

"And amazing," I added, wincing as he slid his cock free before he switched our positions so my head was snuggled into his chest.

"That was really fucking amazing," he confirmed, placing a gentle kiss on my forehead. "I don't think we can ever go back to that restaurant, though," he mused, and we both burst into laughter.

"What exactly does being yours mean?" I asked, still panting lightly.

"You belong to me, and no one else gets to touch you. The same way I am yours," he threaded our fingers together as my heart melted.

"So I'm your girlfriend?" I asked, needing to hear it like this, plain and simple, before I let my heart get any deeper into this.

"You are so much more than that to me, but yes, you are my girlfriend," he pressed a soft kiss to my temple. "Mine," he sighed in contentment, and I couldn't help the huge beaming smile that spread across my face.

Painting Gluttony

CHAPTER THIRTY

Laurel

I'm happy in that cheesy, romance novel way, where I could literally skip across the room. Waking up wrapped in Joe's strong arms brought me a sense of peace and contentment that I hadn't known existed until now. As soon as he knew I was awake, he had shifted my hips and slid inside me, giving me two earth-shattering orgasms that had a permanent smile plastered to my face. I had been even more surprised when he insisted on coming to work with me this morning. I had two meetings with potential clients this afternoon and wanted to get everything looking perfect for their arrival. I snuck a glance over my shoulder as I wiped the shelves and caught Joe staring at me with that look that sent shivers through me like I was a beautiful work of art.

"I thought you were here to help me, not distract me." My tone would have sounded more authoritative if I didn't have that huge grin plastered on my face.

"I can't help myself," he told me in that gravelly voice that let me know how aroused he was. Joe crossed the room in three huge strides, pinning me to the bookcase behind me and captured my lips in a kiss that took my breath away.

"Well, well, isn't this touching," called a familiar voice that made the hairs on my arms stand on end.

Abigail.

Abigail was standing inside my waiting area.

She had dyed her hair jet black and cut it to just below her ears. She was wearing yoga pants and a loose t-shirt tied in a knot, showing off her smooth, tanned stomach. She looked completely different, if I hadn't heard her voice, I wouldn't have recognised her.

Painting Gluttony

"Abigail, what are you doing here?" Joe demanded, still holding me against the bookcase like he could protect me from her. The smile that crossed the other woman's face made a chill run through my veins. We both watched her turn and lock my front door before facing us with glee written across her features.

"I just wanted to come and check in with my soon-to-be ex-husband," she shrugged, starting to walk around the room, looking at everything with disgust once more. "I figured he would have taken our house back, but nope, it's sitting empty." Joe released me from the wall but stayed in front of me, keeping himself between me and Abigail. "Which tells me he's shacking up with someone else." I saw Joe had discreetly turned his phone towards me on the opposite side of where Abigail was standing. The sneaky devil had dialled 999 a few minutes ago, and they were listening to us and hopefully sending help. We just needed to keep her here and keep her talking.

"Mrs Hamilton, what can we do for you? I thought the police arrested you?" I tried to keep my voice as even as possible, I didn't want to give this bitch the satisfaction of seeing me scared of her.

"Of course they didn't. They were far too late," she told us, walking closer to us. I tugged myself free of Joes' grip, and he reluctantly released me, allowing me to stand in front of him so he could keep the call going. "I need cash so I can get set up comfortably somewhere else."

"Won't Henry help you out?" Joe snapped, and it took me a minute to realise Henry was the solicitor Abigail had brought with her, whom Joe thought she was sleeping with. Abigail frowned like she wasn't expecting him to ask that, and Joe snorted a laugh." He didn't want to be linked to any of your illegal activity, so he cut ties with you, didn't he?" His laugh seemed to enrage Abigail, and she lashed out at my reception desk, slamming her fist down on it and swiping all the contents off its surface—like a toddler having a tantrum.

"I need your help, Joe. I'm still your wife!" she screamed, her eyes took on a slightly unhinged look. I was about to open my mouth when my front door suddenly crashed in towards us, no match for the battering ram brandished by two uniformed police officers.

"Stop right now!" Was shouted by a male voice, and we all instinctively froze. Three armed Policemen piled in and were stood where my door used to be, in full protective gear, and their guns caused a shiver to run down my spine. "Everyone is going to slowly stand up and raise your hands into the air," he ordered.

"Fuck this," Abigail snarled and reached above my head for the dropped letter opener, and it was like the world went into slow motion. Her arm pulled back as she readied her strike on me, but then Joe grabbed her other arm to pull her off me. The weapon sliced through the air and impaled straight into Joes' stomach. We all stared at the site of the wound as she withdrew the letter opener, now covered in blood. Crimson spread out across his stomach and began to pour down his jeans. He pressed his hand to the wound, but one of the officers knocked it away as they reached for Abigail, trying to restrain her as she screeched and swiped manically at anyone who got close to her. Joes' eyes bored into mine for a few seconds before his knees gave out, and he collapsed onto the floor.

There was a scuffle going on around me, but I couldn't take it in—I was transfixed by Joes' eyes fluttering closed as I crawled across the floor to his body that had gone frighteningly still.

"Joe!" I screamed, shaking him to try and keep him awake. His eyelids fluttered, and I screamed again.

"Put pressure on the wound!" A voice called to me through the scuffle. I looked around frantically but couldn't see anything useful, so I pulled off my pale grey cardigan, messily folded it up and pushed it onto where the blood was pouring out of Joes' side. He roared in pain, and his eyes flickered open.

"Don't you dare give up on me!" I told him, but his eyes fluttered closed again making me scream and increase the pressure. A voice finally broke through my panic.

"This is all your fault!" Abigail snarled at me as two officers struggled to get her out the door despite her hands cuffed behind her back. Gone was the perfectly put-together woman I had been intimidated by all those weeks ago, in her place was a woman with a vendetta, her hair in disarray and a crazed look in her eyes. "If you had just left us alone, none of this would have happened! None of it! You bring trouble wherever you go, Laurel, and I am going to make you pay for bringing it to my door!" She screeched as she was finally carried out the door by the Policemen.

Painting Gluttony

Her words had made me feel even more guilty because they were true. No matter what I do or where I go, I always seemed to attract trouble and chaos. I kept the pressure on Joes' wound with my ruined cardigan as another officer told me the ambulance was just pulling up. I just hoped it wasn't not too late for Joe to recover and break free of me.

CHAPTER THIRTY-ONE

Laurel

I have always hated the smell of hospitals. I know no one really likes that smell but I always associated it with something bad happening to me. Joe needed to have scans and then stitches on his stab wound so I had been in the waiting room for hours, with nothing to do but think about my arse going numb on the hard plastic chair and what Abigail had said to me. Did Joe even want me here right now? Or was he done with me and my drama? Finally, a nurse came to the waiting room and told me I could go and see Joe. She showed me to his room and then bustled off. I knocked on the door hesitantly, unsure if he wanted me to be here.

"Come in," he called, sounding tired. I tip-toed into the small, private room, and closed the door behind me, completely unprepared for Joe's appearance. He looked physically and mentally drained, and he had dark circles around his bloodshot eyes as he cradled his left arm to his injured side.

"What did the doctor say?" I ask as I inch nervously towards the bed.

"They are keeping me in overnight as a precaution, but the knife missed my organs, so I should be completely fine in a few weeks," he told me with a tired smile.

"I'm glad you're going to be okay," I mumbled.

"Yeah, that crazy bitch is finally gone for good, but she had to get one last swipe at me," he sighed, and his hand instinctively went to his injured side again.

"I don't want you to go through this again," I began to tell him, my voice cracked slightly.

"Abigail is going to prison for a long time, Laurel. You don't need to worry," Joe reached over for my hand, but I took a step away from the bed and out of his reach. "What's happening right now?" He demanded.

"I think I should go," I mumbled, not wanting to say the words, but I forced them out anyway.

"What the fuck, Laurel?" Joe snarled, and I flinched from his anger.

"I think you would be better off without me, trouble follows me around like a bad smell, and I don't want to put you through that." I looked down at the hospital bedding because I couldn't look at his face. If I look at him, I would change my mind and be selfish, and I would never leave his side. I heard Joe rise from the bed and stalk towards me, but I still couldn't look at him.

"Look at me, Laurel," he snapped, and I instantly I found myself lost in his stormy eyes. "Wearing that necklace means you're mine," he gently gripped my throat, and God help me—I was getting aroused when I was supposed to be breaking up with him. "I will decide when we are over, and I am far from done with you," he snarled and spun me around as he bent me over the bed. His hand slid over the bare skin of my thigh as he tugged my dress up and left my backside exposed in my tiny thong.

Painting Gluttony

"The door and blinds are closed, so relax and take your punishment, Laurel," he whispered near the shell of my ear and made me shiver in anticipation. Spanks rained down on my arse, delivered harshly and made me moan at the heady combination of pleasure and pain, and I burrowed my face into the sheets to try and quieten myself. Joe finally stopped, and his hand moved under my drenched thong, where he gently tapped my clit, and drove me to the edge of an intense orgasm. Just as I was about to fly over the edge, he ceased moving and backed away.

"What the hell?" I cried as I whirled to face him, not caring that my dress was still up around my waist and my hair was probably everywhere from writhing on the bed.

"Punishment for doubting me," he smirked. "If my side wasn't being held together by stitches right now I would fuck that message into you too. Instead, why don't you come and take care of your boyfriend?" I was on my knees on the hard linoleum floor when his words caught up to me.

"Boyfriend?" I asked dumbly as he threw off the hospital gown. I took in each toned part of his body before lowering to his hard cock—the head wept for me already. He had never called himself that before.

"Yes," he said. He gripped my hair as he pulled me towards him and pushed his cock into my mouth in a silent order. An order I was all too happy to obey, allowing him to fuck my face how he liked as tears ran down my cheeks and saliva dripped from the corners of my mouth, and I didn't care because I had never been more aroused than at this moment. His grip tightened on my hair, and I knew he was close, so I reached one of my hands up and squeezed his balls. Joe jerked in surprise before he filled my mouth and throat with his release.

"Good girl," he praised me, running his hands soothingly through my hair. "Now, don't you dare ever think of running off like that again. Ever." He looked down at me with such adoration that it made me feel warm and whole. I didn't know what I was thinking, trying to walk away from him. He accepted me for who I was and gave me anything and everything I needed.

"Yes, Sir," I agreed.

EPILOGUE

Joe

Two months later...

"Just a little further," I coaxed Laurel forwards, my hands covering her eyes as I walked behind her and guided her towards her office. I was nervous about giving this gift to Laurel—my other gifts to her hadn't always been well received, but this one I hoped she would like. It was odd, but I had never felt nervous about showing someone my artwork before. Normally I felt confident in what I had created, and if they didn't like it, that was their problem, but this painting of Laurel was different. I felt like I had poured my soul into this one, and I was laying it bare for her to see and risk her rejection. We hadn't said the L word yet, and I was nowhere near ready to say that word out loud, but I felt like this painting said it for me. I dropped my hands from her eyes and studied her face for her reaction.

In front of us was a painting of Laurel. My original one of her was lost when my studio was trashed, and the police had no leads on who it was, so I had to start over. When I started to paint again, I wanted this piece to be different from all my other work. This was something that was going to be just for Laurel, to show her how much she meant to me.

She gasped and clapped her hands over her mouth, and her eyes went watery. Oh shit. I thought she hated it. I have painted her with that strong and powerful look she gets, wearing her hair loose and that damn black dress I loved so much. I wanted to show her the feistiness and beauty that I saw inside her every day.

Painting Gluttony

"It's so beautiful," she finally said, making me sag with relief. "I look so beautiful. Thank you, Joe," she spun around and wrapped me in a tight hug.

"With your new business helping women in need, I figured you might need a constant reminder of how I see you in your office," I explained. Laurel pulled back slightly and studied my face for a moment.

"I feel the same way," she told me with an affectionate smile and my heart nearly bursts. She understood.

The End

Erin Coal

Painting Gluttony

There are tonnes of books out there to choose from, so thank you so much for choosing this one- it really means the world to me ❤️☐

My name is Erin Coal, and I have dreamt of being a writer since I was a little girl. Lockdown 2020 finally gave me the shove to make my dream a reality. I am addicted to pizza, love watching the Jacksonville Jaguars play and spend most of my free time with my husband and our ever-increasing number of pets! ☐

I write about real, smart, and sassy heroines who find their happily ever after with a sexy alpha male. Their journeys are often messy and complicated, but love will always find a way in my world ❤️☐

Thank you again for choosing to support an indie author ☐☐

If you loved or even hated this book, then I would love to hear from you:

Website: www.erincoal.com
Instagram: erincoalauthor
Email: erin.coal@hotmail.com

Erin Coal

Turn the page for a preview of Solving Greed, the third book in Erin Coal's Seven Deadly Sins series.

Erin Coal

Painting Gluttony

CHAPTER ONE

My heart is hammering in my chest, beating out it's erratic rhythm that echoes in my ears. I need to relax, but I just can't. I have wanted to achieve the rank of Detective Constable for as long as I could remember, and here I was on my first assignment, and it was an undercover one, too, so the pressure was really on. My second-hand Doc Martens squeezed my feet painfully as I walked, and the jeans and crop top I was instructed to wear let a cold autumn breeze caress my stomach. Even though I had a leather jacket over the top, I felt too exposed. I much preferred to wear my armour of formal clothes that kept me covered and hidden. My blonde hair was floating loose around my shoulders, and I itched to tie it back into a bun and out of the way.

"Name?" A gruff-looking man demanded from me, sitting behind a camping table that had seen better days. Being honest, so had the man himself, everything about him looked worn and tired.

"Tiffany Stevens," I told him, sounding much more confident than I felt giving him the fake name. My real name, Sophie Gove, was on the tip of my tongue. He scanned his clipboard before finding my fake name there, nodding, and crossing me off. He handed me an auction paddle and scrutinised my face for a few seconds before motioning me to proceed through the metal detectors. My body urged me to run, my skin itching from the man's gaze, my anxiety telling me that he somehow knew I wasn't supposed to be there.

I tossed my car keys and the auction paddle into a tray and passed through the body scanner without issue, the envelope of hundreds in cash burning a hole in my jacket pocket. I hadn't bothered to bring my phone as I knew there were signal jammers all over this abandoned warehouse to stop any details of the items from leaving the auction room before sales were finalised. It's understandable. If you were going to host an auction of stolen and illegal goods, you would want people to pay and leave before the police got wind of it. Too bad the police were already here, aka, me.

The auction room itself was really just a huge, abandoned warehouse that still had puddles of standing water on the floor and discarded paper strewn around from when the previous owners left. A few of the leftover chairs had been placed into rows to create a makeshift audience area, but the stability of them looked questionable, so I moved to stand near the back of the large room. I scanned around, taking in the handful of buyers spread out around the room. No one spoke to each other, probably because no one trusted each other. My eyes landed on a man lounging back leisurely in his chair, his legs crossed and placed on top of the back of the chair in front of him, like he was above all of this. He sensed my eyes on him, and he turned to face me. Holy crap, he was hot. His olive skin and deep brown eyes made my stomach give a pleasant flip-flop before he shot me a scowl and turned around again. Dick.

Without his face to distract me I swept my gaze over his body. His shoulders and thighs looked muscular and huge, bulging against his jeans and leather jacket, that made me drool slightly. Damn. Physically he was just my type, but mentally he was an arsehole.

"Let's get this show on the road," calls an authoritative male voice. A man strides into the room and takes his position at the front. His jeans and Fleetwood Mac t-shirt look well worn, enhanced by the deep wrinkles around his beady eyes and his grey-blonde hair that is swept back off his head. I suspect it might be hiding a bald spot on top. In his arms was a huge rifle, the wooden grip reflected the strip lights above, and the ebony barrel looked thin and lethal even from the back of the room. "Item one is an antique hunting rifle. All distinguishing markings have been removed, and it is in full working order. Let's start bidding at one hundred pounds."

Several paddles hit the air. I had known it was going to be hard to sit here and watch crimes being committed or planned, but I could never have imagined it would be this hard. I was having to suppress my every instinct not to try and stop the sale and arrest everyone for taking part. The rifle eventually sold for seven hundred pounds. I shuddered to think what it was going to be used for, nothing good that's for sure. Several other lots passed by, including a pen drive containing people's bank information and some diamond jewellery, before what I came here for was finally brought to the front.

"Item ten is sketches believed to be by a famous artist. No authenticity confirmed, but these were acquired from the artist's private studio." I knew what acquired meant. It was a fancy way of saying they were stolen. "We will start the bidding at fifty pounds." Only three paddles hit the air this time, clearly not much interest in art here, and the auctioneer pointed towards the gorgeous arsehole, "I have fifty here... do I have sixty?" I raised my own paddle, trying to keep my hand as steady as possible despite my frayed nerves causing a slight shake. Someone else got their paddle up first, but gorgeous arsehole still turned to scowl at me, and goddamn it, I even thought his scowl was hot. What was his problem?

As the bidding reached a hundred and fifty pounds, the other two bidders had dropped out, so it was just me and the gorgeous arsehole. We were glaring at each other across the room with a tension that could be cut with a knife, neither of us looking at the auctioneer as we continued to raise our paddles, refusing to back down. I don't know why this guy got under my skin so much, but I wanted to beat him in this auction more than I wanted to prove myself as a police officer right now.

"Do I have one sixty?" The auctioneer called. I raised my paddle, throwing out a look of what I hoped came across as haughty defiance.

"Three hundred," called gorgeous arsehole. His voice was gravelly and seductive and made my lower body clench. Fuck, even his voice turned me on.

"Do I have three ten?" The auctioneer looked at me expectantly, but I was fucked. I only have two hundred in cash on me. If the arsehole hadn't been bidding, I would have won this at a hundred. Fuck him. I lowered my eyes to the floor in defeat and shook my head to indicate I was out. "Sold for three hundred." Fuck. My first undercover assignment, and I wasn't going to deliver on it.

Two more lots went by in a blur while I started at my boots and tried to formulate a plan to get this operation back on track.

"Item thirteen is a twenty-two-calibre handgun. It is in working order but still has the serial numbers, so buy at your own risk. Can I get twenty-five pounds?" My paddle is in the air before I even think it through properly. I need to buy something in order to blend in and keep my cover in case I need it for next time, so why not take a gun off the street in the process? "I have twenty-five... can I get thirty?" A man on one of the chairs near the front raises his paddle, and I restrain myself from throwing something at him in frustration.

"Fifty pounds," I call out, cutting off the auctioneer and drawing a couple of curious glances.

"Any advance on fifty?" He calls out to the room. No one moves. "Sold for fifty," he points at me, and I give a tiny sigh of relief.

There are only two more lots after that, a watch and a tiny spy camera, and then everyone starts moving to collect the items they won and hand over the cash. It all seems surprisingly civilised for a place where guns and stolen items are sold. As I queue up for my gun, I restrain myself from arresting the guy who bought the antique rifle while he stands in front of me, inspecting his purchase before handing over the cash. If I can, I need to get his car license plate later so my colleagues can keep tabs on him. Instead, my eyes scan the room, catching sight of a gorgeous arsehole walking towards the door with some papers sealed in protective plastic. Fuck. I needed those.

Rifle guy finally pays up and moves on, and it's my turn to collect. I thrust the cash at the bewildered man facilitating the exchange and grab the gun without checking it, thrusting it into my jacket pocket and giving chase to the arsehole who bought my art.

"Wait!" I call, chasing after the annoying Adonis into the dimly lit car park. He turns to face me with one eyebrow raised.

"Or what? You'll shoot me with your traceable gun?" He nods to the obvious bulge in my jacket pocket, and I shift uncomfortably. "Buying stolen art and a gun no sane criminal would want," he leans in, close to whisper the last words to me, "you couldn't be more obviously a cop, sweetheart." The way he calls me sweetheart is scathing and condescending and riles my anger up again, but his gravelly voice also has my nipples pebbling, which is too goddamn confusing to think about right now. He rolls his eyes at me and heads further across the parking lot.

"I need to buy that art from you," I chase after him, burying my anger in my desperation. "I'll give you double what you paid." He freezes with his fingers over the handle of the driver's door of his car.

"The art isn't for sale," comes a new male voice that sends a shiver of fear through me. A figure comes into view just behind the arsehole, a complete opposite of him in every way. My eyes are immediately drawn to a jagged scar running from the corner of the new guy's left eye to the corner of his mouth. I gulp as I think about the ways he might have gotten that. The new guy is massive and not in the muscular way that I like, his designer suit stretched taut around him. The streetlight reflects off his bald head as he takes his time looking at me from head to toe. His eyes are so cold I shiver slightly.

"I like your little friend Logan. What's your name, sweetheart?" The way he calls me that makes my skin crawl, every sense telling me this is a really bad guy, and I should be as far away as possible, but at least I know the other arsehole's name is Logan now.

"Tiffany, and who are you?" I try and force a flirtatious smile onto my face. Logan shoots me a scowl. I ignore him, as if being nice to this creep gets me the art I need, then I really don't care what he thinks.

"For now, just call me 'Boss'," the new guy grins at me. "Now, Tiffany, I am very sorry, but the sketches aren't for sale, even to a girl as pretty as you." He peruses my body again shamelessly, and I fight back the urge to wrap my arms around myself protectively.

"I think she's desperate. She offered to pay double what I got it for," Logan puts in, and it's my turn to scowl. Boss seems to consider this a moment.

"Tell me, Tiffany, what are you planning on doing with that gun?" Boss asks, nodding towards my pocket. Crap. I need to think on my feet.

"I owe someone big time. There was a finder's fee for that art, that's why I was here. I had the idea in there that I could rob someone to get the cash I need if your man here wouldn't let me buy it," I shrug as if this is no big deal.

"You weren't planning on stealing from me, were you?" Boss' tone takes on an icy edge that freezes my heart for a few seconds. Shit, that was probably the worst lie I could have given him, now he thinks my agenda was to take the art from Logan at gunpoint..

Painting Gluttony

"I've no bullets yet," I shrug, aiming for sarcasm to get me out of this, and Boss bursts out laughing.

"I knew I liked you," he smirks at me. "Logan, Tiffany and her little gun are going on your next job with you. Think of it as an audition."

"I don't think she's what we need in our group," Logan glares daggers at me, and I pray he won't out me as a policewoman. I know Boss by reputation. Every police officer in North Wales does. You name a crime this guy has been associated with it. I wouldn't put it past Boss to kill me at this point if he found out what I was.

"Nonsense," Boss waves away Logan's concern. "She should fit right in. Besides, if she doesn't, at least she will be pretty to look at for a little while." His thinly veiled threat makes my stomach clench in fear, but I keep the look of haughty indifference glued to my face. "Be seeing you real soon, Tiff." They both get into the car and leave as I stand and watch, my face blank. A one-time undercover task has just become a longer-term thing. Fucking perfect. I can't wait to pass this on to my arsehole new partner and hear about how I'm a failure. Fuck.

CHAPTER TWO

I almost backed out of going out again tonight and threw myself a pity party at home instead. If it had been any other night, I probably would have, but tonight was for charity, so I sucked up my shitty day and shoved it to the side for the night. So, what if my superior now wanted me to be undercover long-term? So, what if she suspected 'Boss' ran a huge smuggling and theft operation and was suspected of several murders? While she had told me all this, my partner had smirked at me like the arrogant arsehole he is, and said nothing to back me up. Tonight was a charity submissive auction at a local BDSM club, Seven Deadly Sins, and that's what I needed to focus on right now.

I was introduced to the place about six months ago when my colleague Hayden fell in love with a famous erotica writer who uses the club as her inspiration for her books. I became fast friends with his new girlfriend, Amy, and had been slowly dipping my toe into the clubs lifestyle. Tonight, I was launching myself into the fucking deep end.

Amy had introduced me to a friend of a friend, Bella, who had been slowly teaching me how to be a submissive. Things like what safe words to use, what to look for in a Dom and standard things all Doms would expect, so I finally felt ready to find a Dom of my own and give this a real shot.

The rules of the auction tonight were simple; each of the seven submissives that had volunteered for this had agreed to spend 10 hours with the Dom that won them. We had all listed our turn-ons and hard nos, which would be listed in a small paper booklet. After the auction, we would sit with our Doms to discuss details and terms. It all sounded so easy when it was put like that, but my hand was still shaking as I swiped my membership card to gain access to the club masquerading as a warehouse.

I pushed open the door to the changing room, which always reminded me of a gym changing room, with the wooden bench running through the middle. There were hooks above the bench to hang coats and bags on and lockers on all the walls. Off to one side were a few shower cubicles that were always kept surprisingly clean. There were six other submissives getting ready for the auction. Three men and two women I was unfamiliar with, and another woman I had met a couple of times in passing.

"Hi, Sophie," she smiles and waves at me. She's gorgeous with long red hair that skims her bum and a perfect hourglass figure that I envied.

"Hi, Natalie," I respond, throwing my backpack onto the bench, "are you nervous?"

"Nah, this is going to be a blast," she grins, touching up her bright lipstick in one of the mirrors. She's wearing an emerald green satin nightie that kind of makes her look like Poison Ivy. I'm envious of her confidence, and it makes my nerves slightly worse.

Painting Gluttony

"Are you excited?" Amy asks, sneaking into the changing room and standing beside me, beaming with pride like she's my Mum and it's graduation day.

"I'm terrified," I admit with a grimace, "I don't know why I let you guys talk me into this."

"Hey, come on, you will be fine. It's all going to be great. You're beautiful and filthy, and any Dom would jump at the chance to get a few hours with you," her words make me crack a smile. Amy is beautiful and kind, petite, with blonde hair and big blue eyes. It's no wonder my friend Hayden can't keep his eyes or hands off her.

"If this goes sideways, I'm holding all of you responsible, though," I sigh as I to remove my coat to change.

"As long as you wear the nightie I picked, it's a deal. Nothing is going sideways if you're wearing that baby!" She grins, and I can't help but join in.

"Fine, now scoot. You're not supposed to be back here," I nudge her playfully as three of the other subs head towards the stage for the auction.

"Fine, fine," she wraps me in a tight hug that warms me inside and calms my nerves a tiny fraction. "You'll do great." She tells me before turning to leave me with my thoughts again.

I slip on the black lace nightie and risk a glimpse at myself in the mirror. Damn, Amy really knew what she was talking about. The strategically placed lace reveals teasing snippets of flesh without actually showing anything. I carefully combed out my hair so it fell in soft waves down my back. I applied a little concealer and lipstick; I'd never been much good at putting on makeup and finally put on the small black heels to complete my outfit. I was quite tall for a woman at five feet ten, and I found people, especially men, seemed intimidated if I wore high heels, to the point I only owned one pair now, just in case.

"Come on, Sophie," Natalie calls from the doorway, and I realise everyone else has left apart from us.

"Coming!" I call, chasing after her towards the main room.

The waiting area set up for us behind the stage is literally some plush red velvet curtains that have been hung from the ceiling with a couple of chairs for us to perch on while we wait. Because I arrived last, I'm going to be auctioned last. So by the time it's my turn, I'm so nervous. I'm sweating excessively and constantly fidgeting.

"Next up is the lovely Sophie," The auctioneer announces to the audience, and the irony that this was my second auction today wasn't lost on me. "Sophie is a fairly new sub seeking an experienced male Dom. Please check her list of turn-ons and hard limits in the brochure, and bidding on her will begin in a few moments."

I peek out from behind the curtain and spot Amy, who gives me a discreet thumbs up and grin.

"Please welcome Sophie to the stage!" The auctioneer calls. I draw in a deep breath before stepping out from behind the curtain and into the dazzling stage lights. Here goes nothing.

SOLVING GREED available on Amazon now.

Printed in Great Britain
by Amazon

41984159R00145